CAT & CAT
ADVENTURES
The Quest for Snacks

SUSIE YI

HARPER alley

An Imprint of HarperCollinsPublishers

Thank you to my family, Jack Gang, Yeon Yi, Man Jae Yi, and Heidi Yi, as well as my wonderful agent, Kathleen Ortiz, and the amazing team at HarperAlley who have made this book possible.

HarperAlley is an imprint of HarperCollins Publishers.
Cat & Cat Adventures: The Quest for Snacks
Copyright © 2021 by Susie Yi.
All rights reserved. Printed in Spain.
No part of this book may be used or reproduced in any manner whatsoever without written permission except in the case of brief quotations embodied in critical articles and reviews. For information address HarperCollins Children's Books, a division of HarperCollins Publishers, 195 Broadway, New York, NY 10007.
www.harperalley.com
Library of Congress Control Number: 2021933139
ISBN 978-0-06-308381-3 — ISBN 978-0-06-308380-6 (pbk.)

The artist used a computer, tablet, and the endless source of energy that only cats sitting in your lap can provide to create the digital illustrations for this book.

Typography by Susie Yi
21 22 23 24 25 EP 10 9 8 7 6 5 4 3 2 1
❖
First Edition

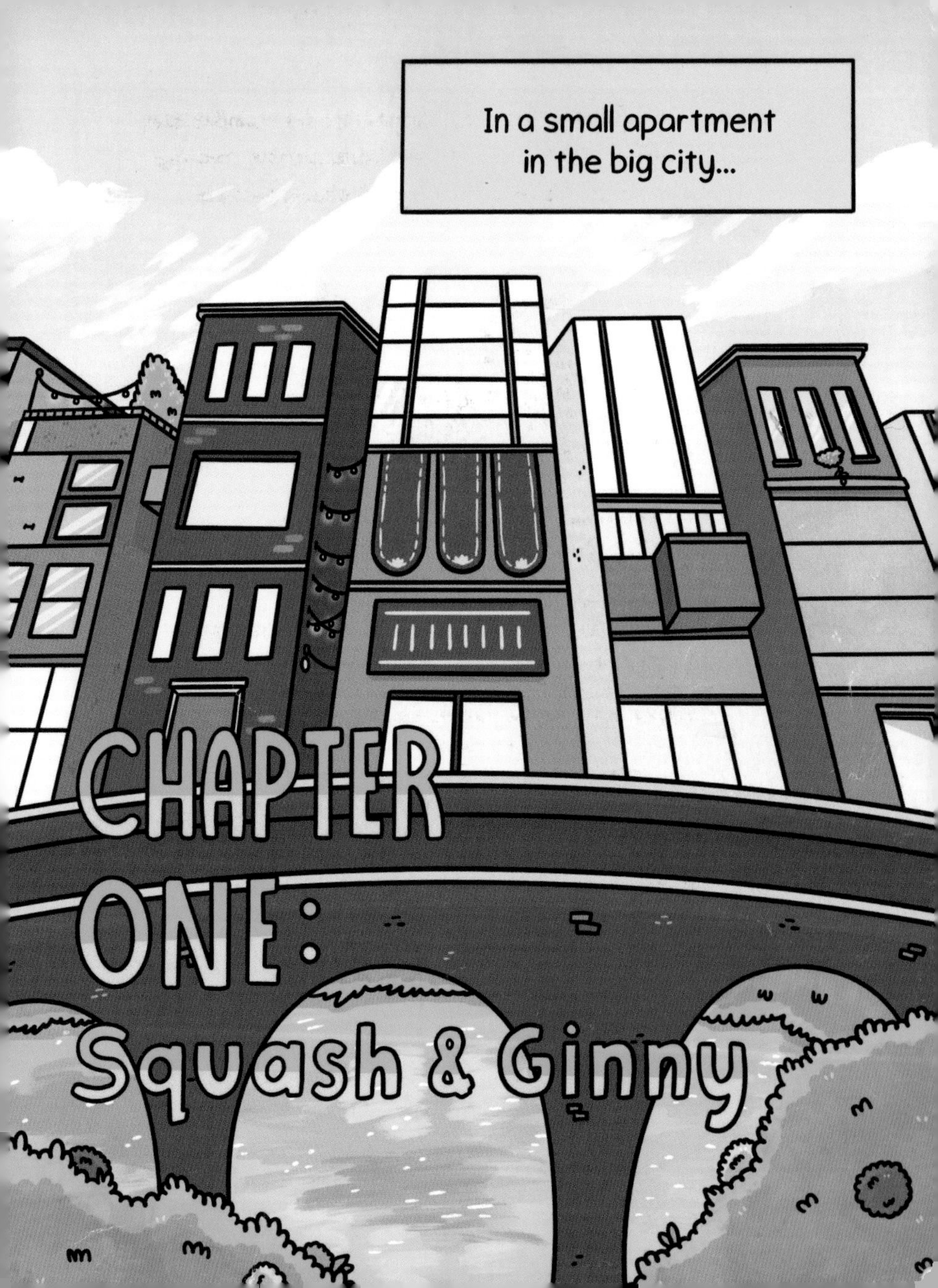
In a small apartment in the big city...
CHAPTER ONE:
Squash & Ginny

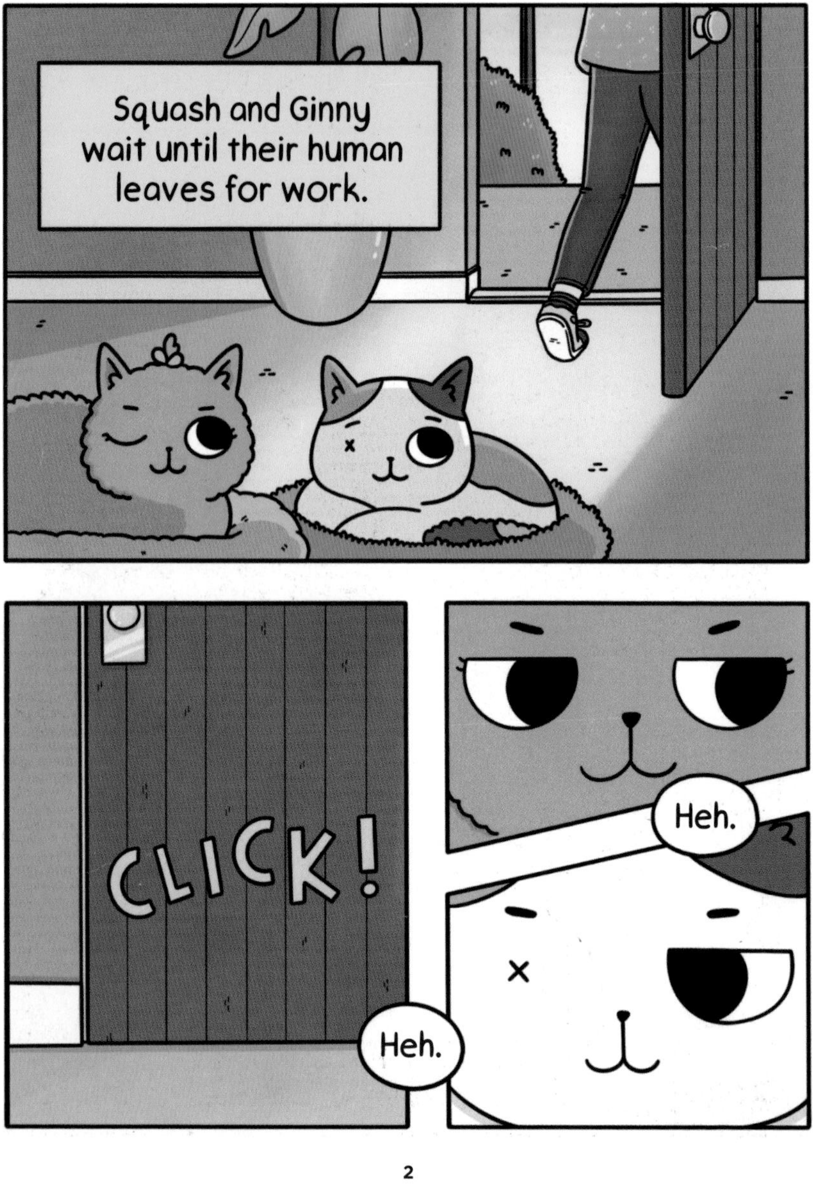
Squash and Ginny wait until their human leaves for work.
CLICK!
Heh.
Heh.

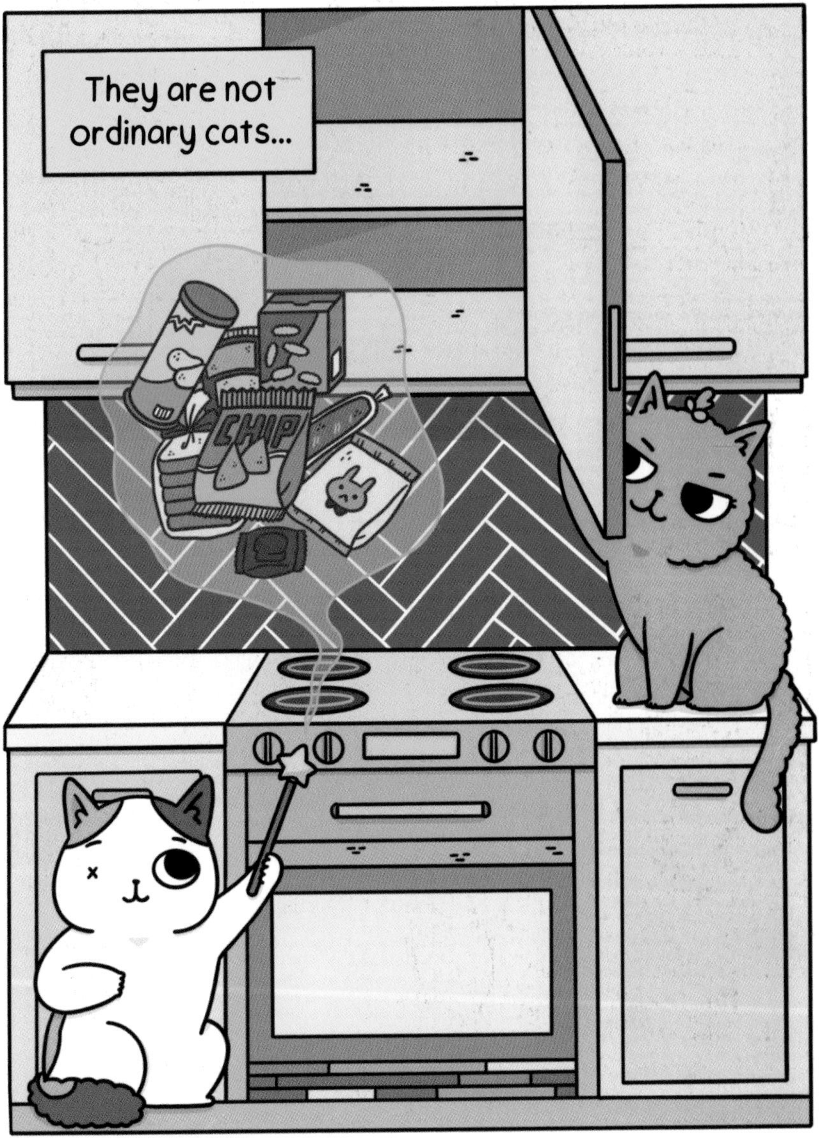
They are not ordinary cats...
CHIP

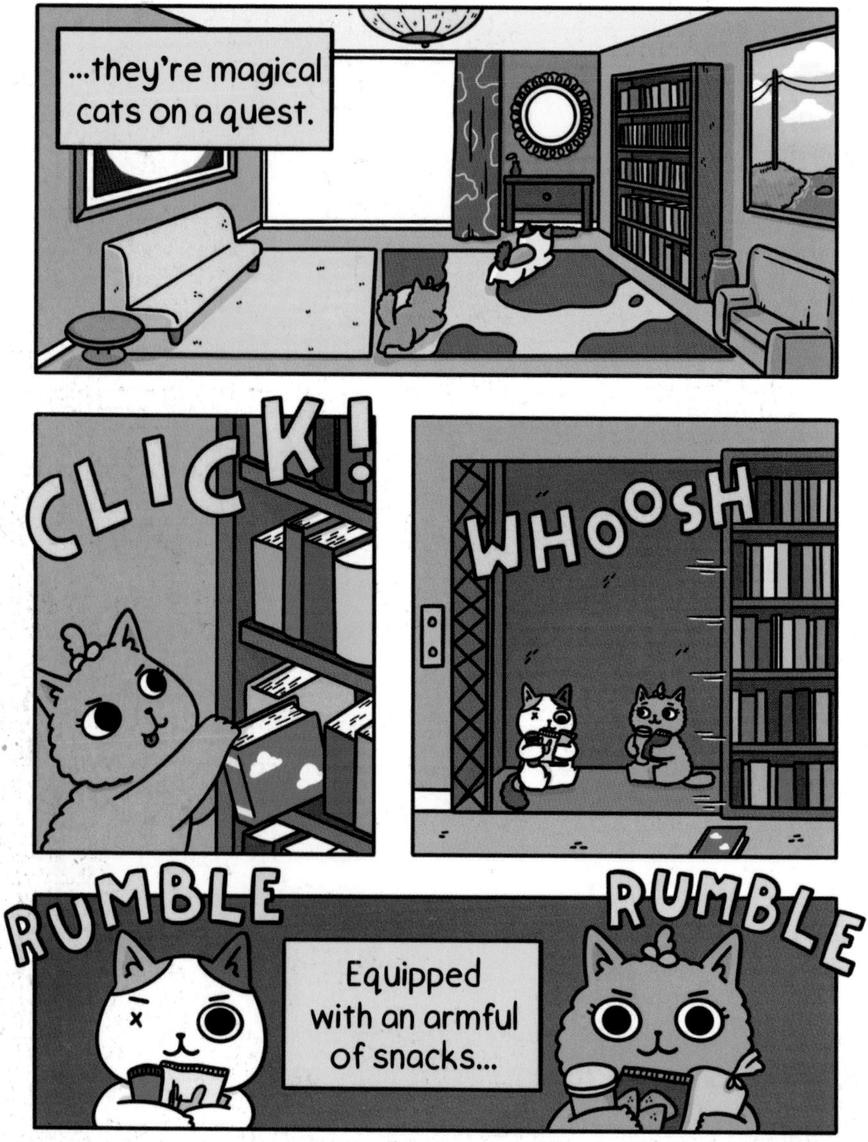
...they're magical cats on a quest.
CLICK!
WHOOSH
RUMBLE
RUMBLE
Equipped with an armful of snacks...

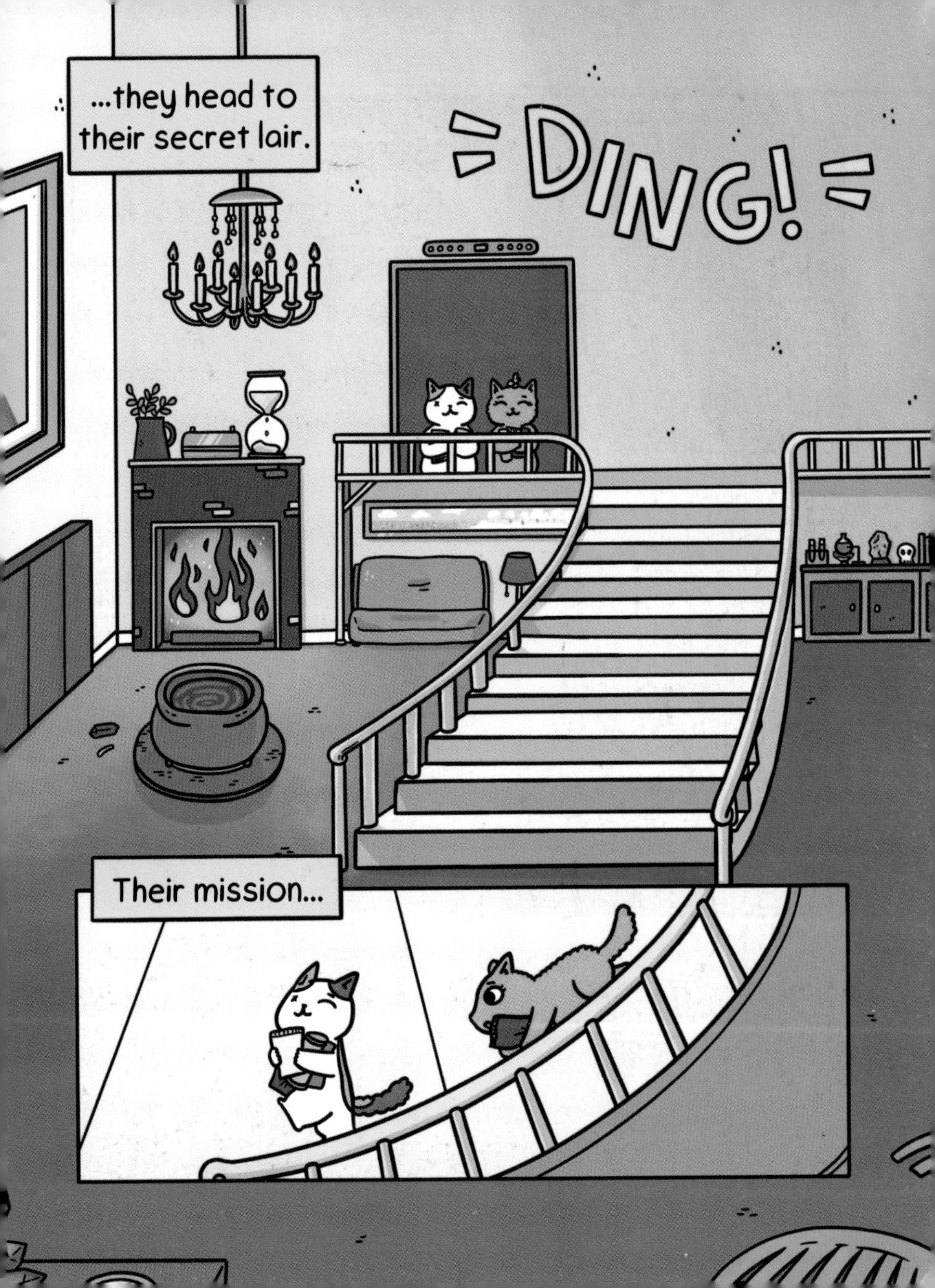
...they head to their secret lair.
DING!
Their mission...

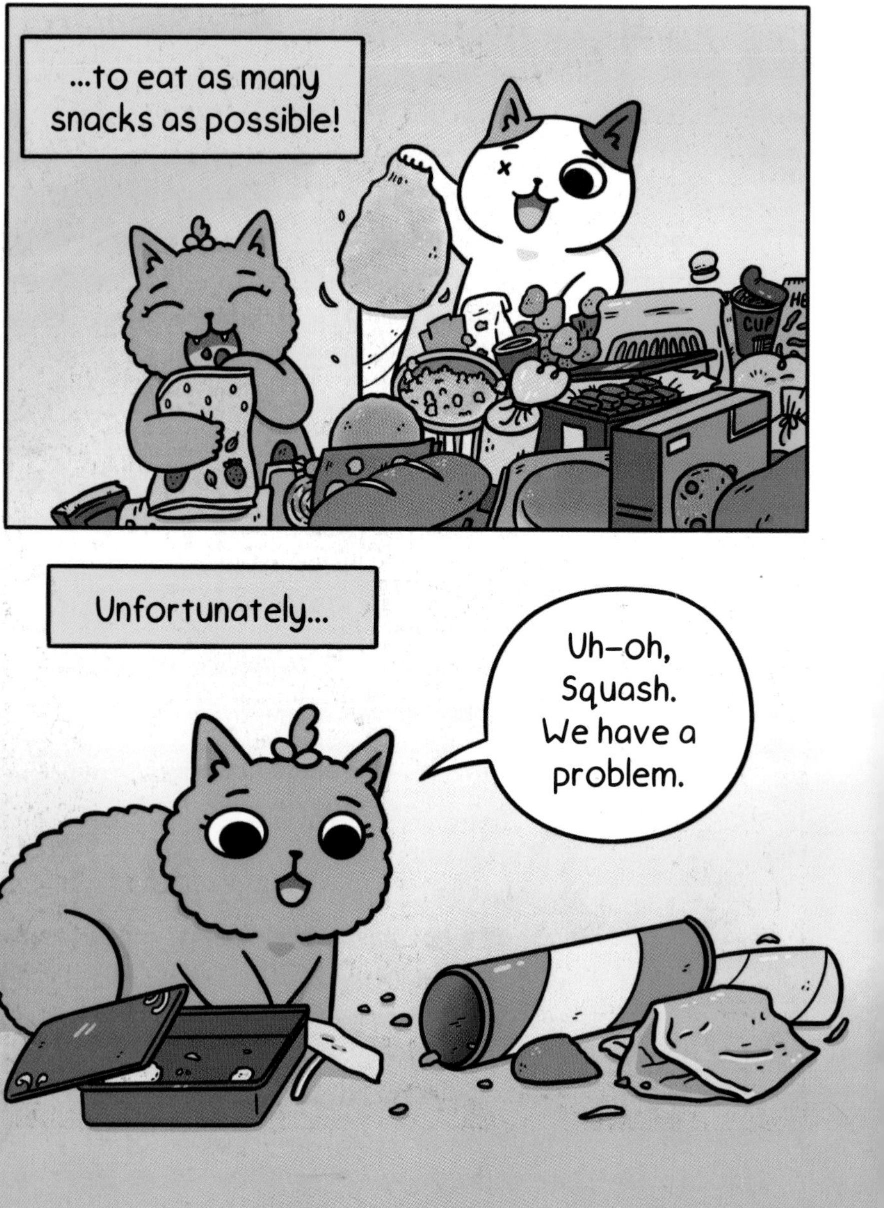
...to eat as many snacks as possible!
CUP
Unfortunately...
Uh-oh, Squash. We have a problem.

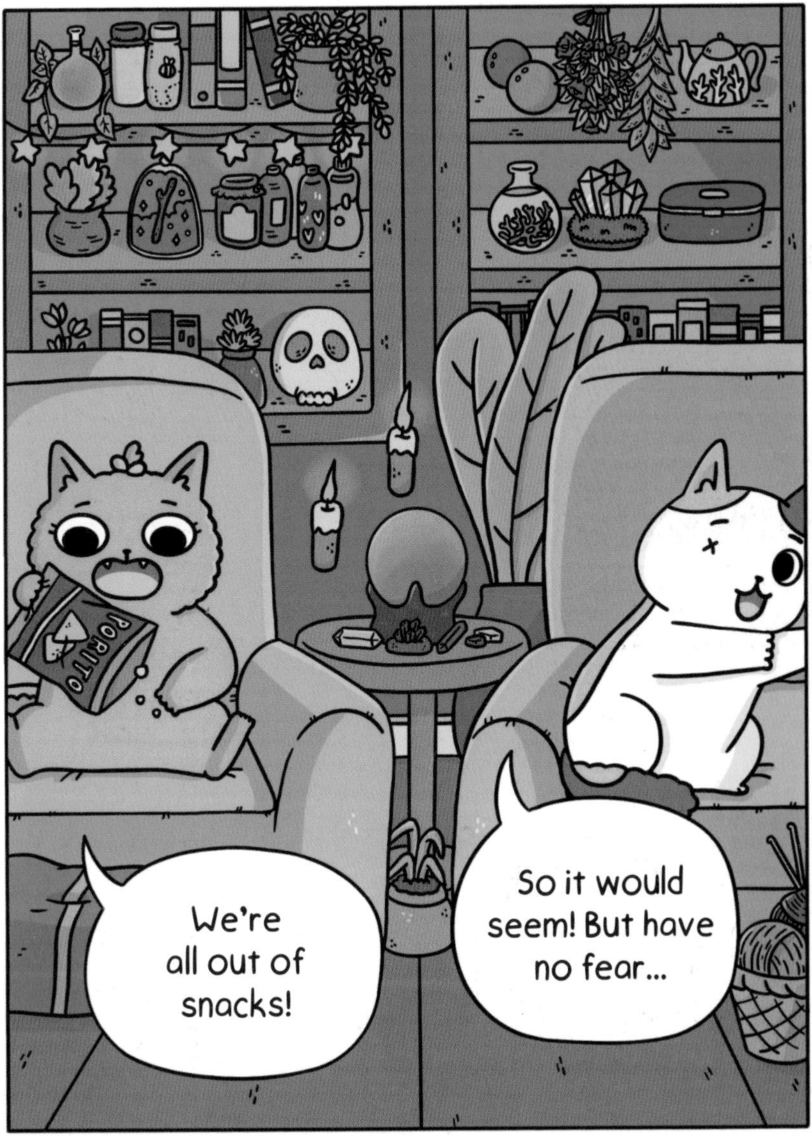
PORITO
We're all out of snacks!
So it would seem! But have no fear...

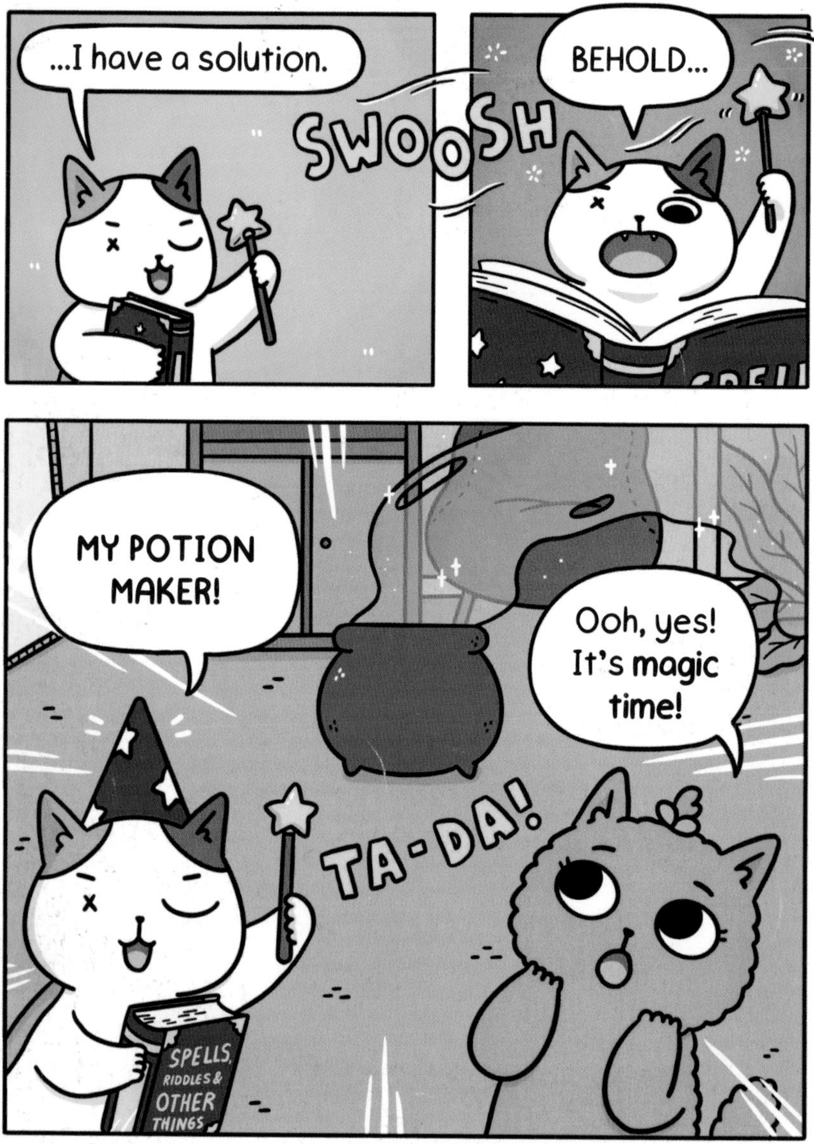
...I have a solution.
BEHOLD...
SWOOSH
MY POTION MAKER!
Ooh, yes! It's magic time!
TA-DA!
SPELLS, RIDDLES & OTHER THINGS

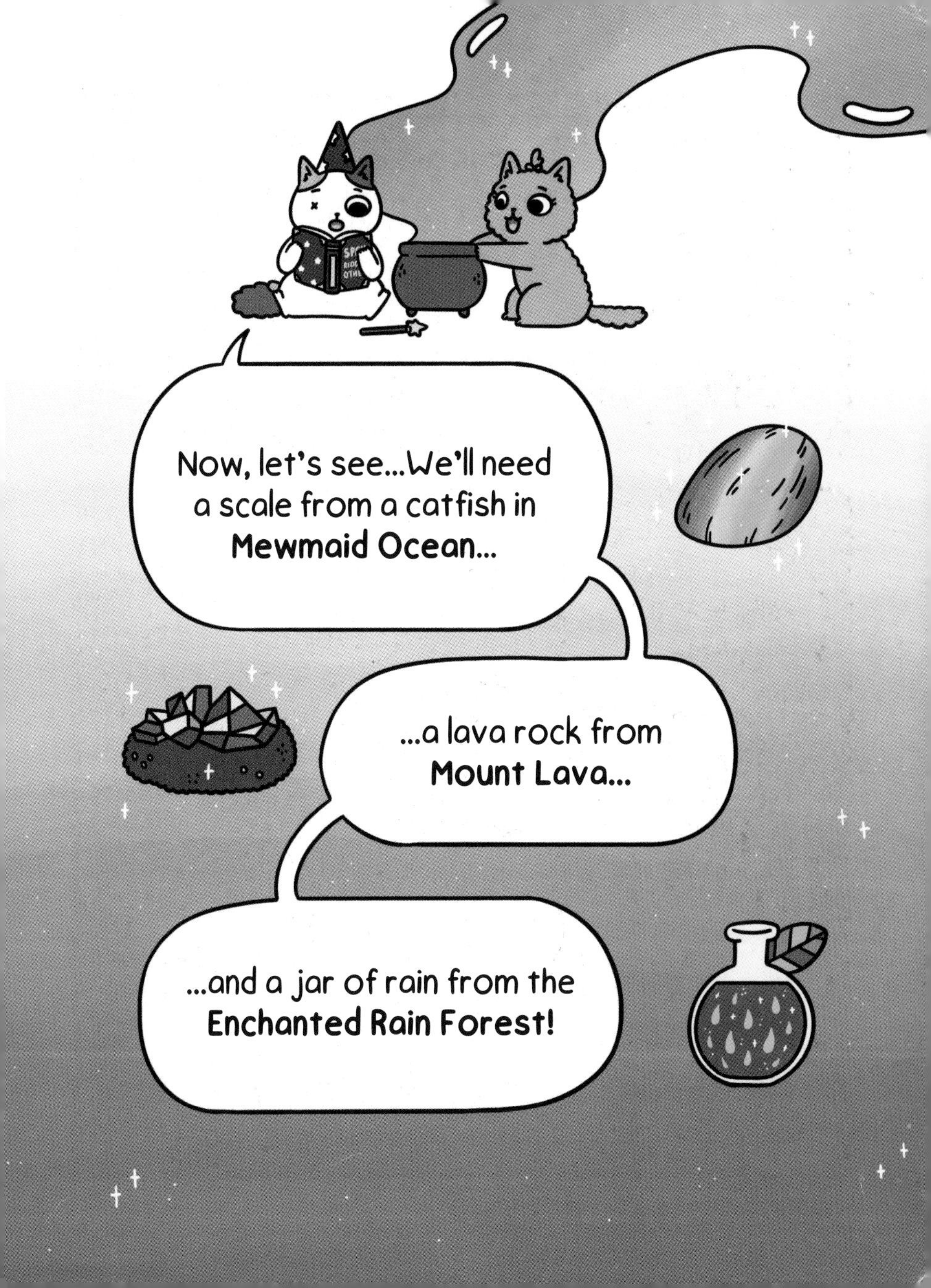

Now, let's see...We'll need a scale from a catfish in **Mewmaid Ocean...**
...a lava rock from **Mount Lava...**
...and a jar of rain from the **Enchanted Rain Forest!**

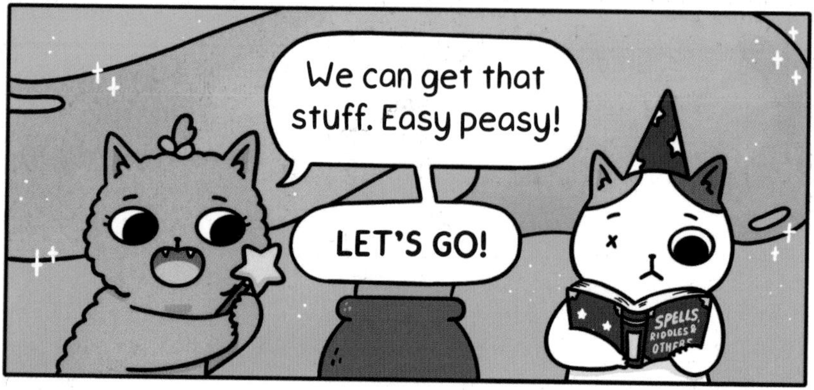
We can get that stuff. Easy peasy!
LET'S GO!
SPELLS, RIDDLES & OTHERS

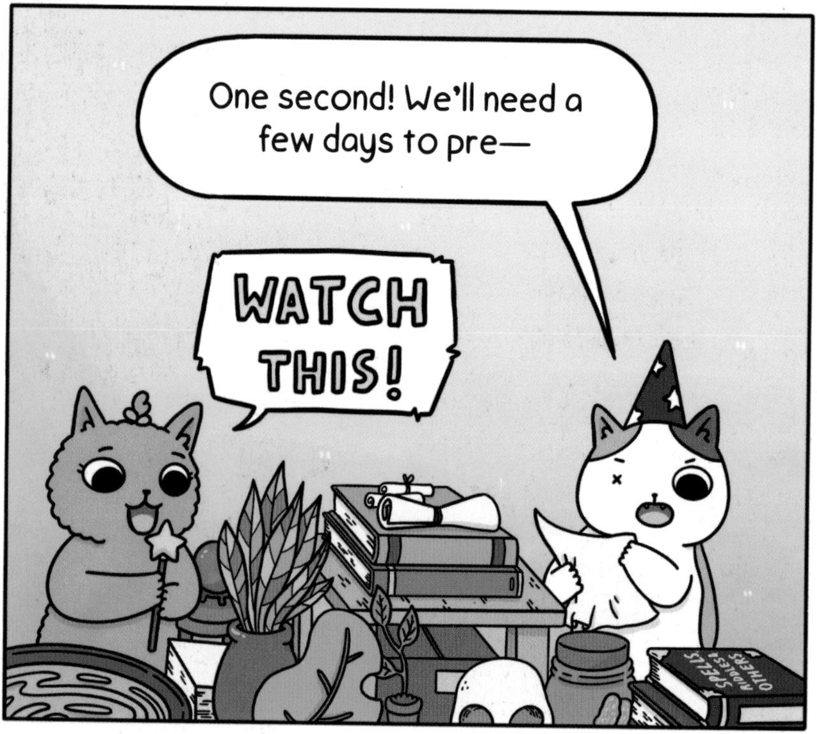
One second! We'll need a few days to pre—
WATCH THIS!
SPELLS, RIDDLES & OTHERS

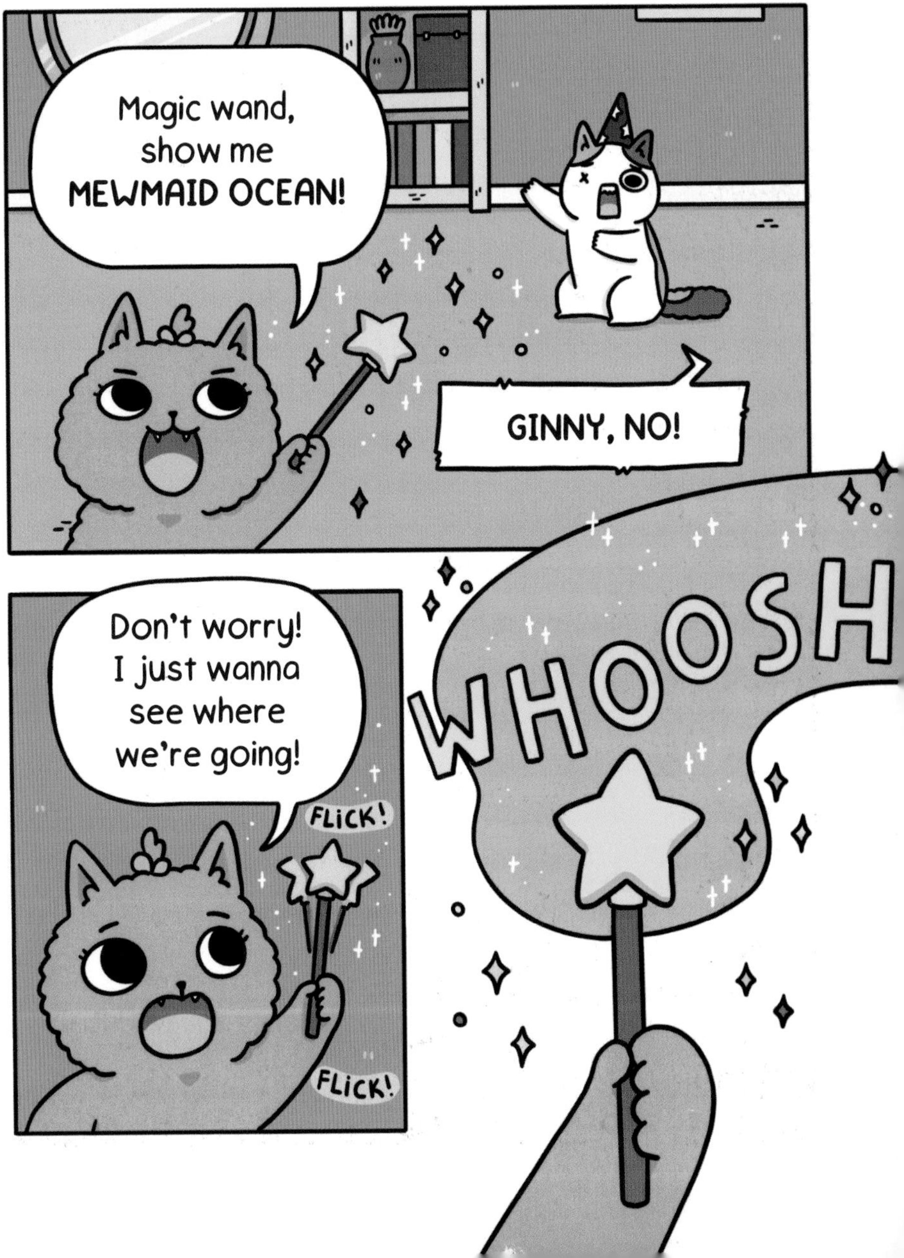
Magic wand, show me MEWMAID OCEAN!
GINNY, NO!
Don't worry! I just wanna see where we're going!
FLICK!
FLICK!
WHOOSH

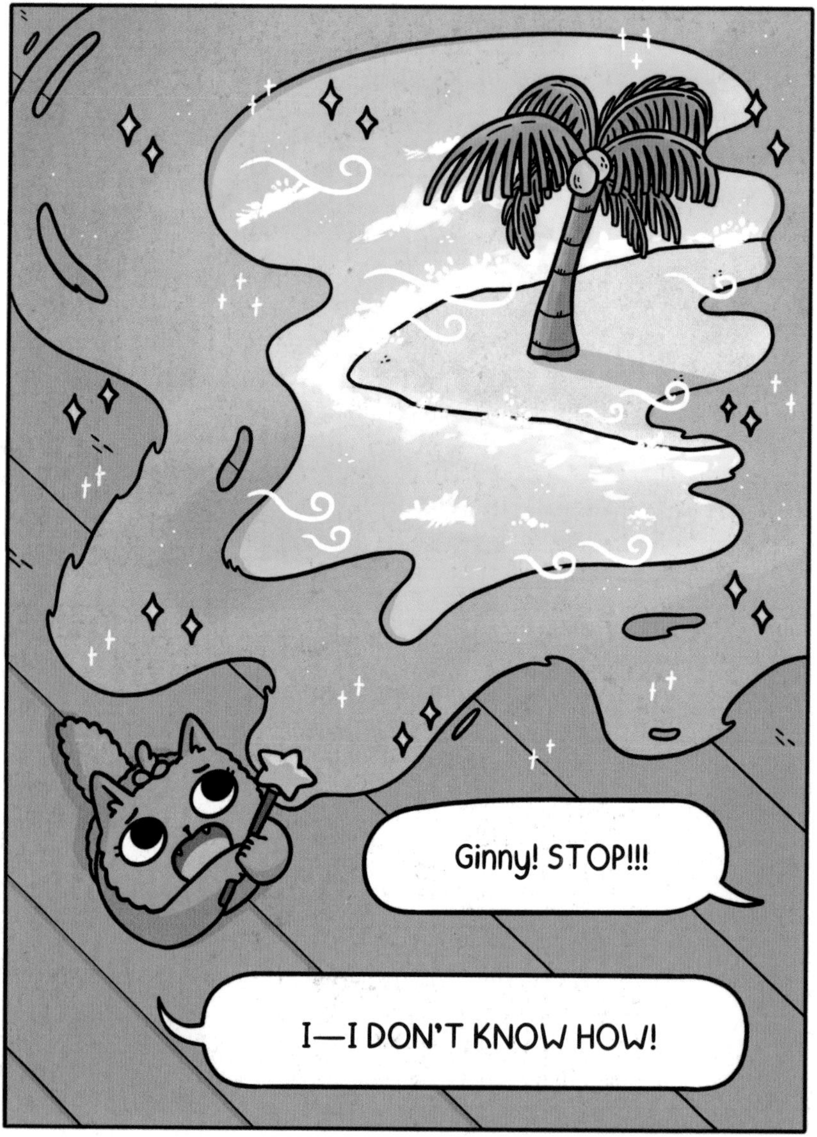
Ginny! STOP!!!
I—I DON'T KNOW HOW!

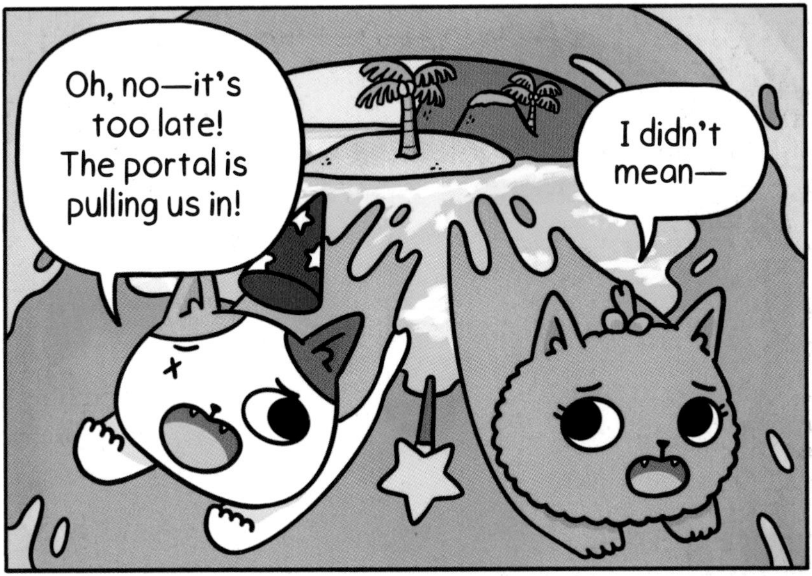
Oh, no—it's too late! The portal is pulling us in!
I didn't mean—

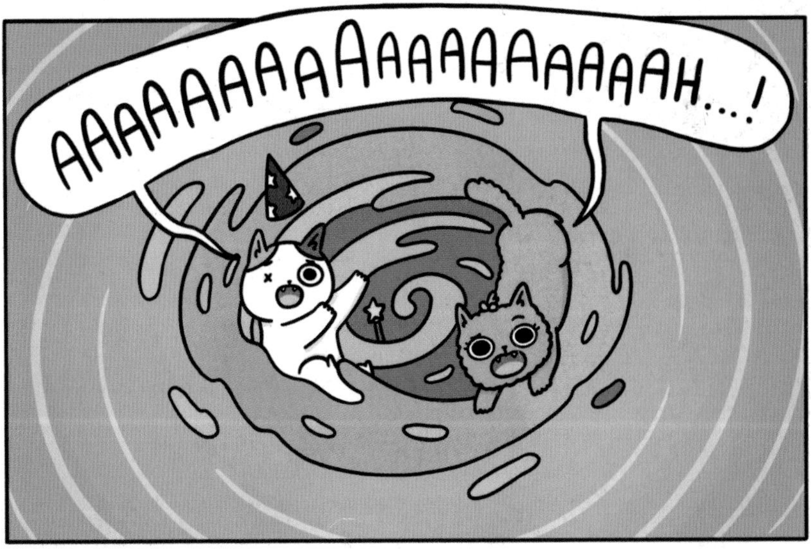
AAAAAAAAAAAAAAAAAAAH...!

PLOP!

CHAPTER TWO: Coral

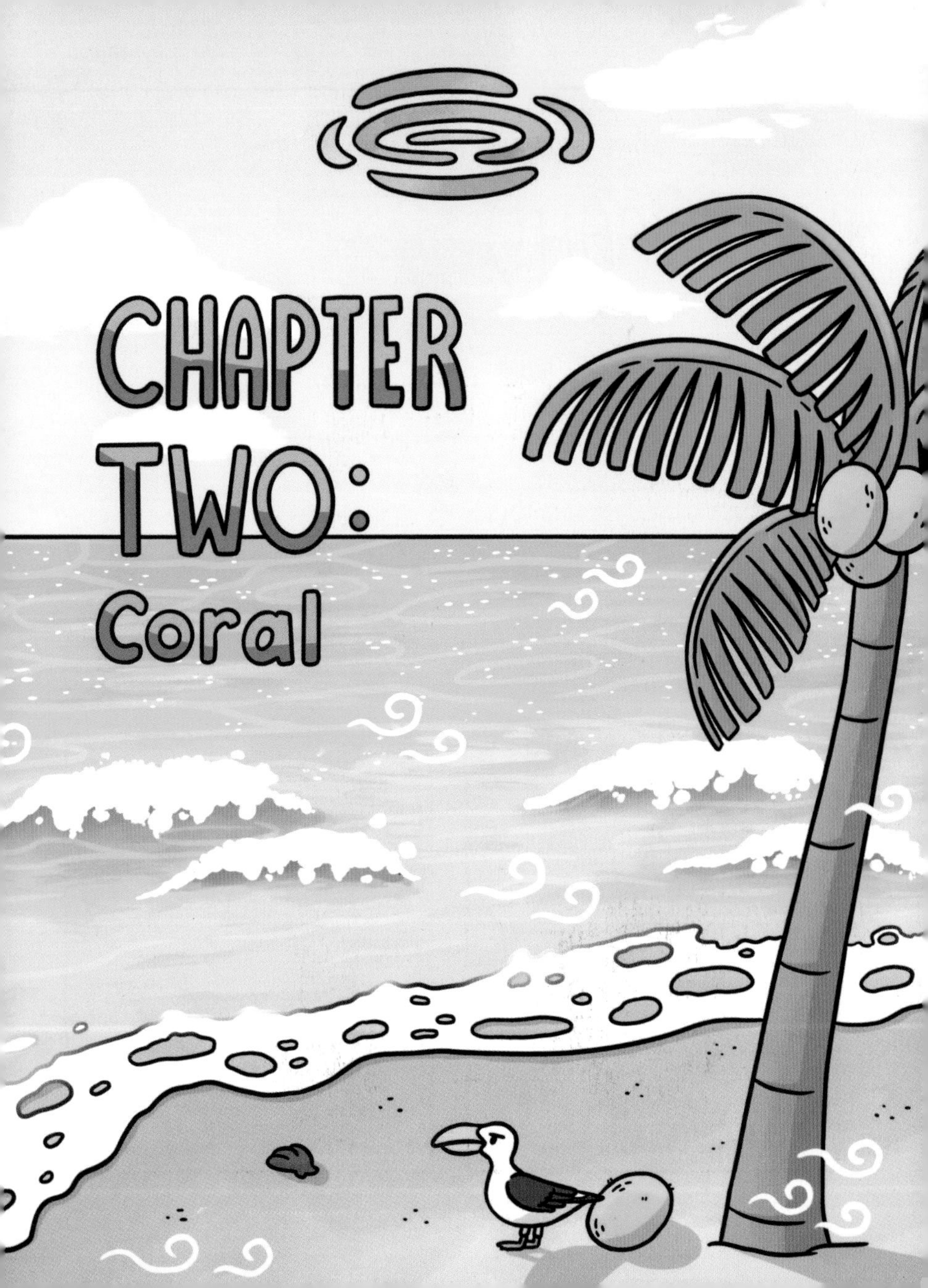

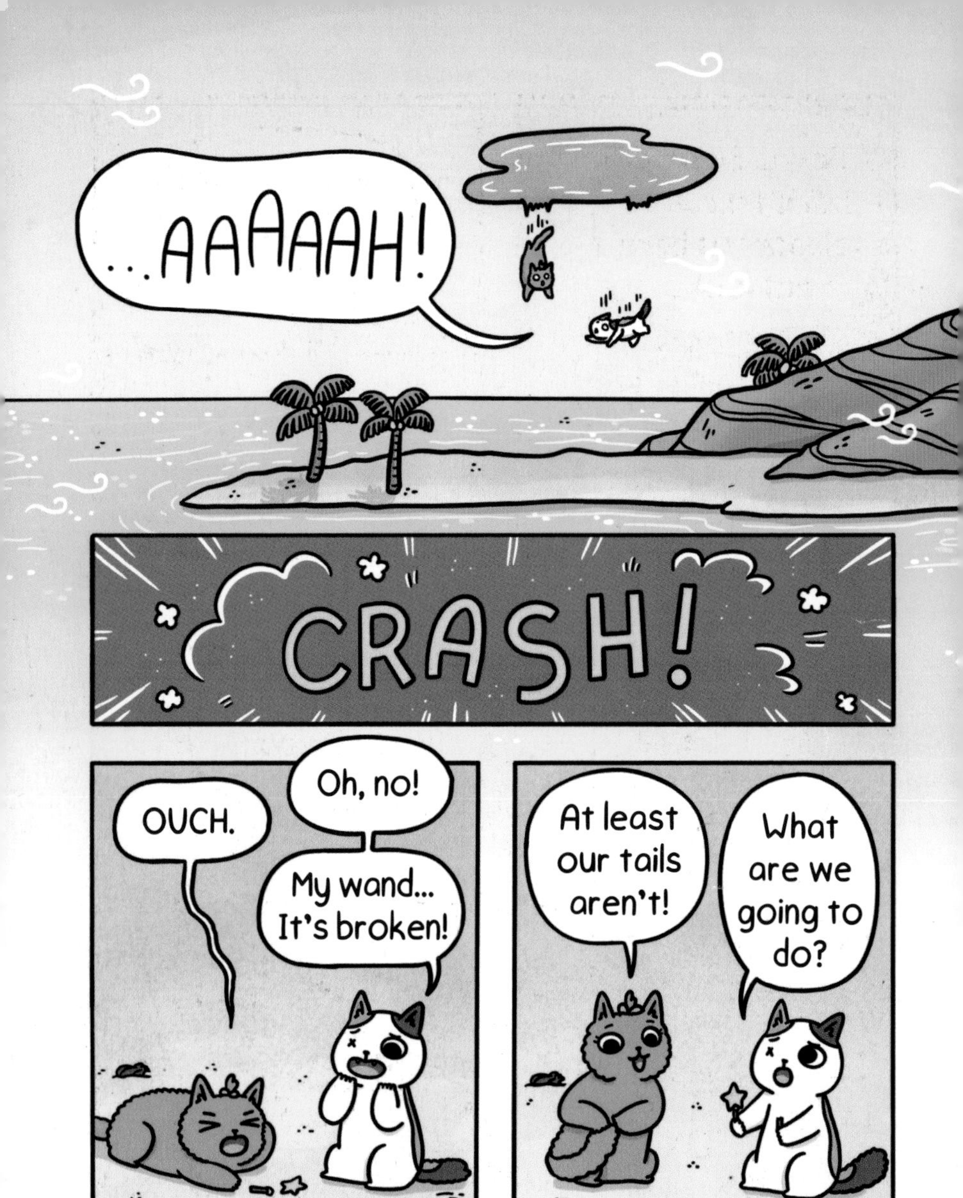
...AAAAAH!
CRASH!
OUCH.
Oh, no!
My wand... It's broken!
At least our tails aren't!
What are we going to do?

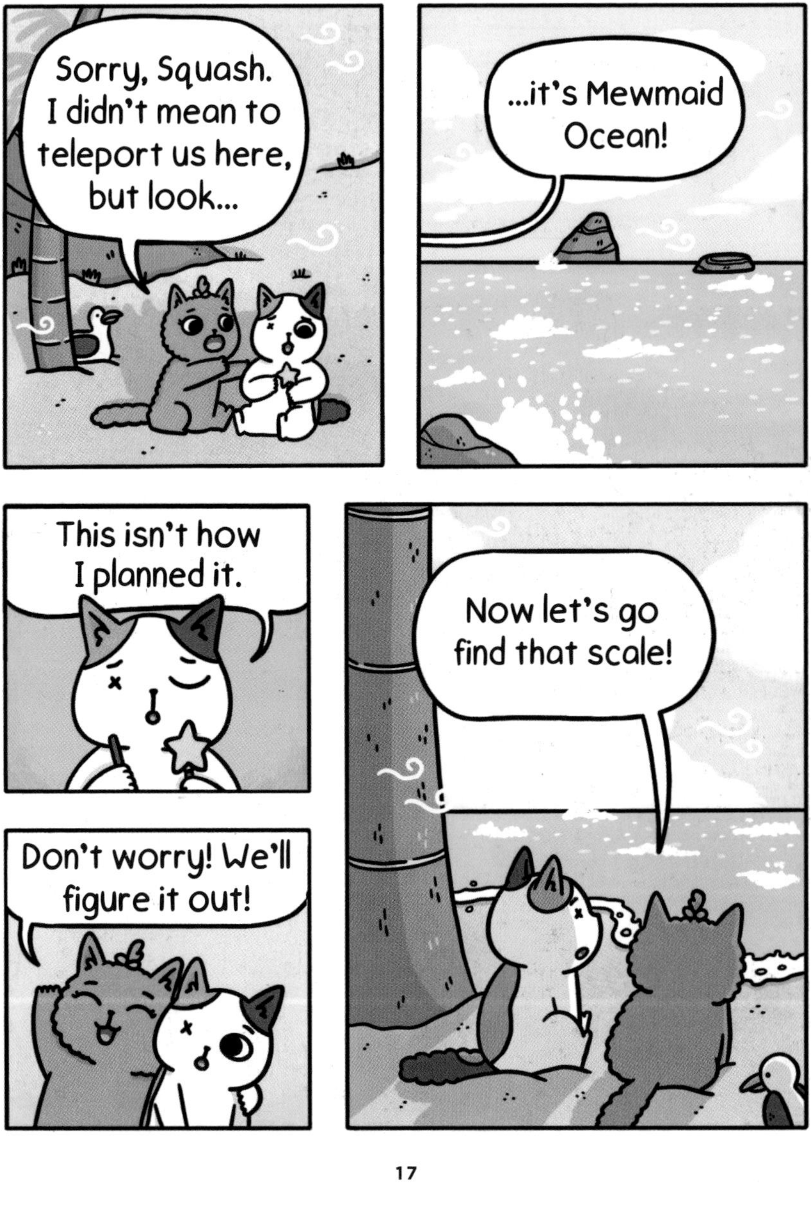
Sorry, Squash. I didn't mean to teleport us here, but look...
...it's Mewmaid Ocean!
This isn't how I planned it.
Don't worry! We'll figure it out!
Now let's go find that scale!

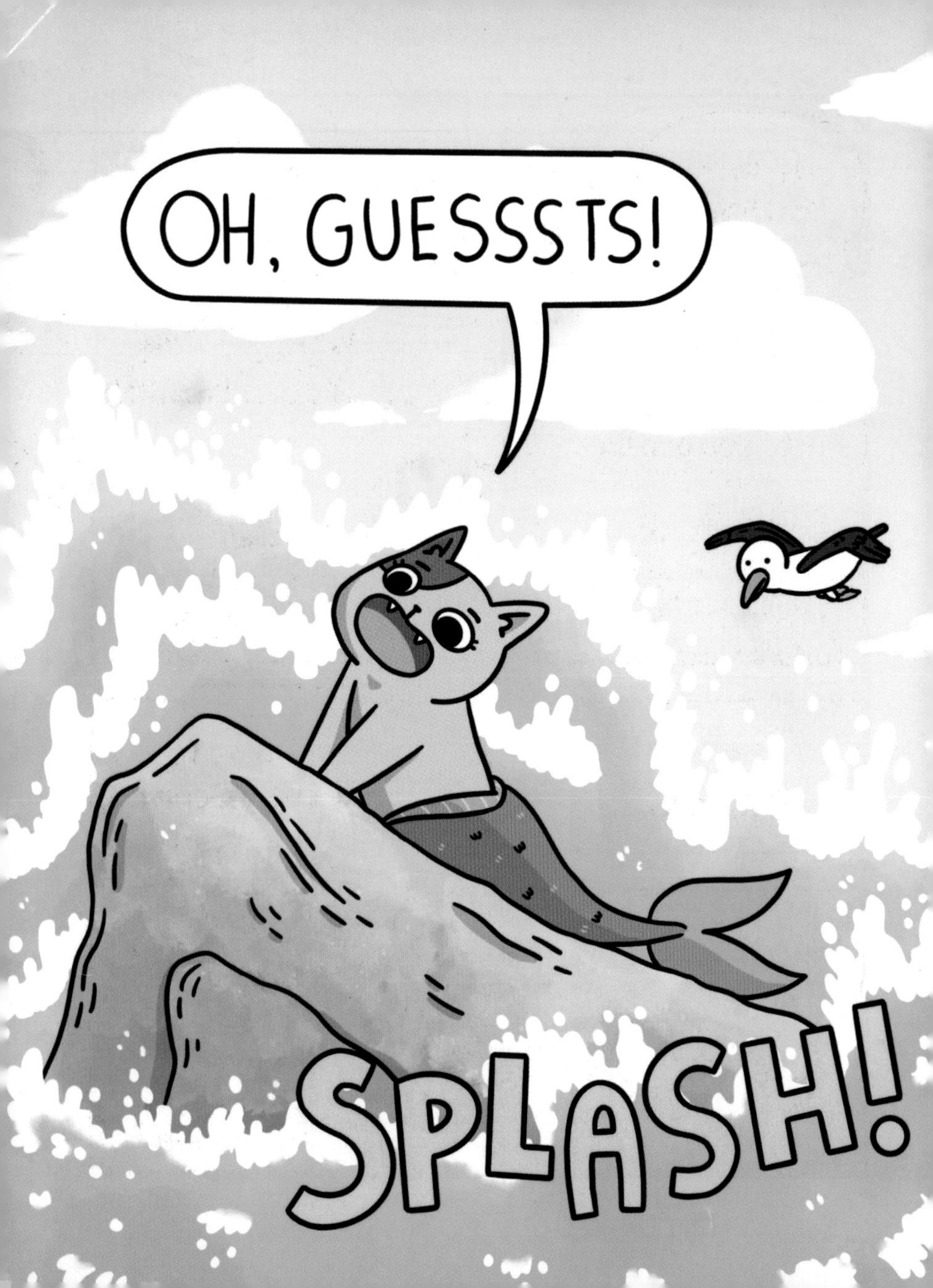
OH, GUESSSTS!
SPLASH!

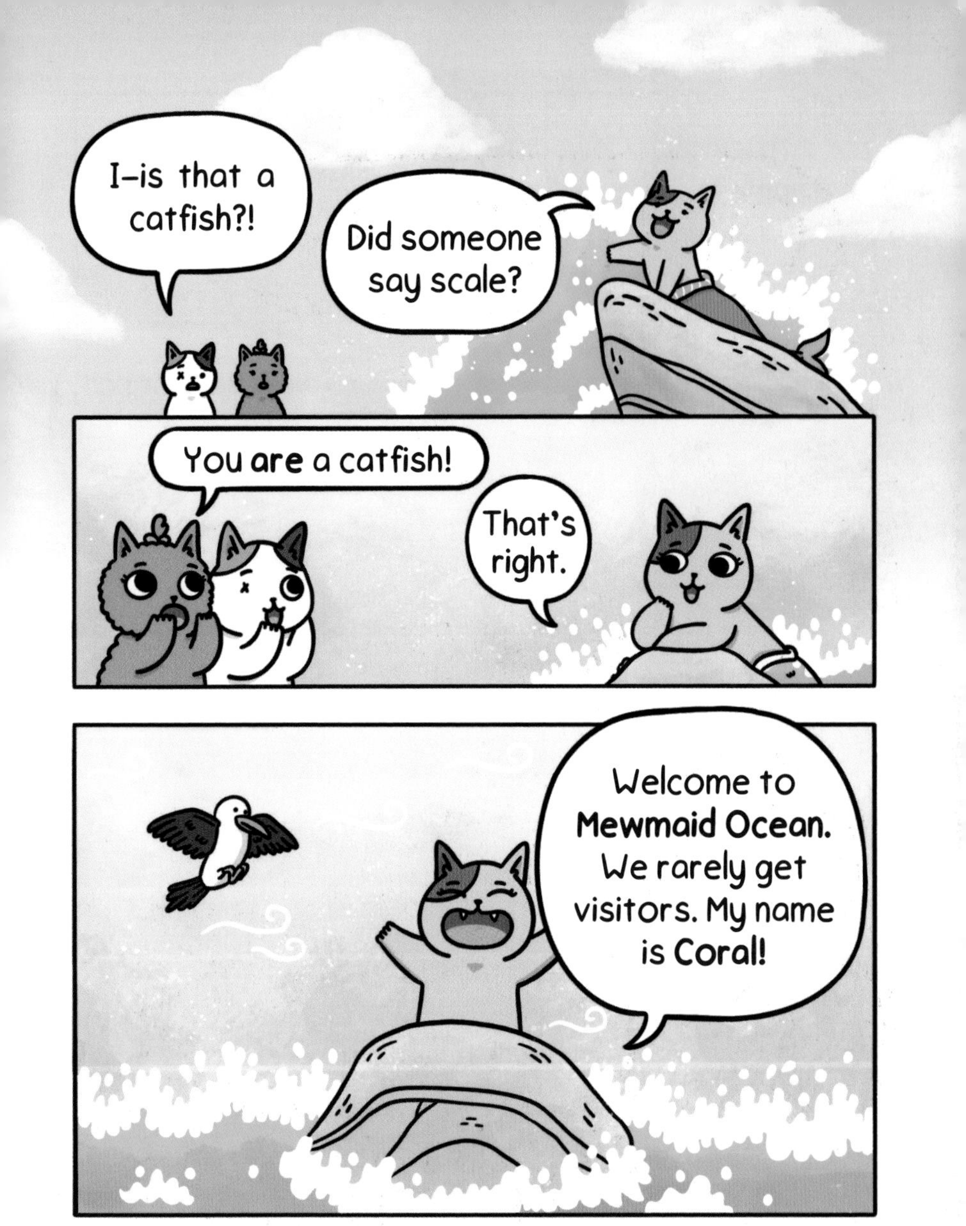
I–is that a catfish?!
Did someone say scale?
You are a catfish!
That's right.
Welcome to Mewmaid Ocean. We rarely get visitors. My name is Coral!

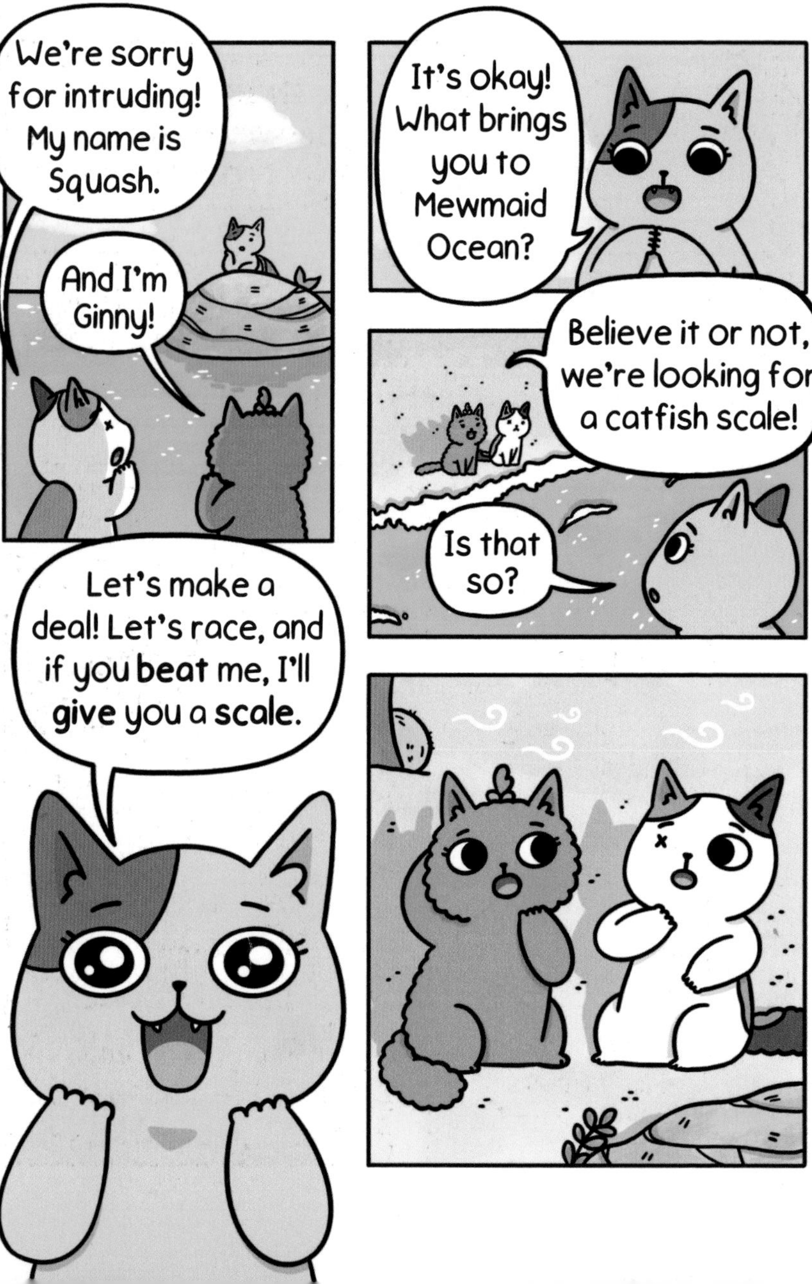
We're sorry for intruding! My name is Squash.
And I'm Ginny!
It's okay! What brings you to Mewmaid Ocean?
Believe it or not, we're looking for a catfish scale!
Is that so?
Let's make a deal! Let's race, and if you **beat** me, I'll **give** you a **scale**.

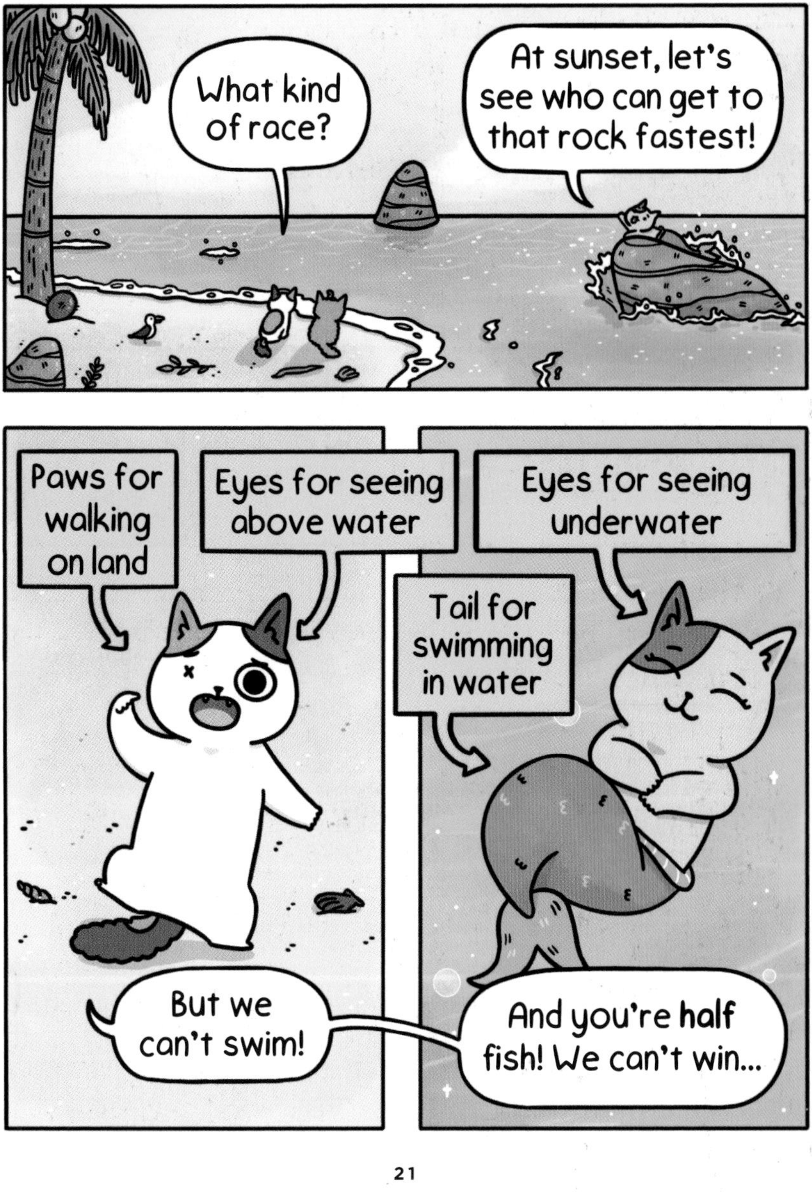
What kind of race?
At sunset, let's see who can get to that rock fastest!
Paws for walking on land
Eyes for seeing above water
Eyes for seeing underwater
Tail for swimming in water
But we can't swim!
And you're **half** fish! We can't win...

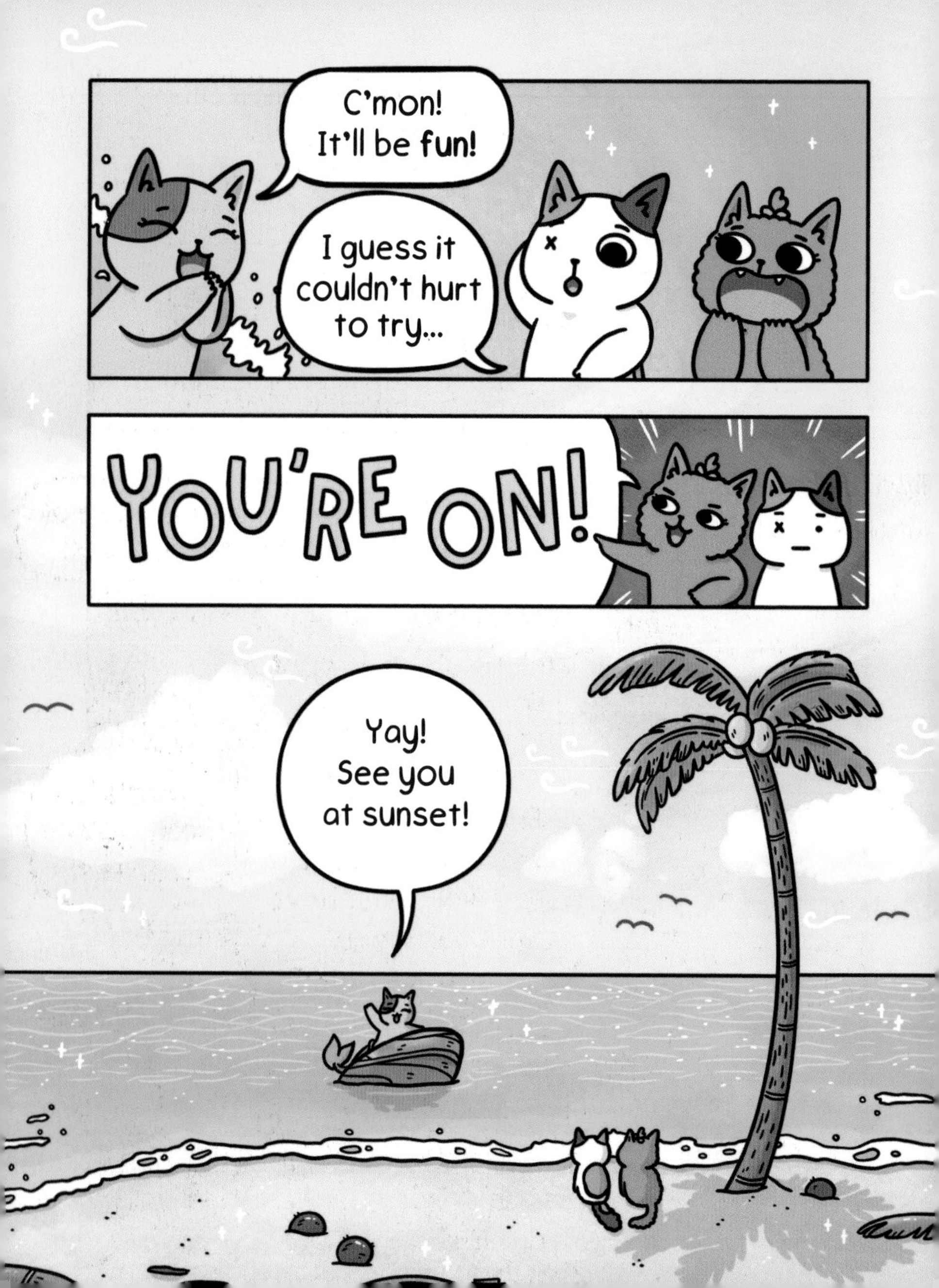
C'mon! It'll be fun!
I guess it couldn't hurt to try...
YOU'RE ON!
Yay! See you at sunset!

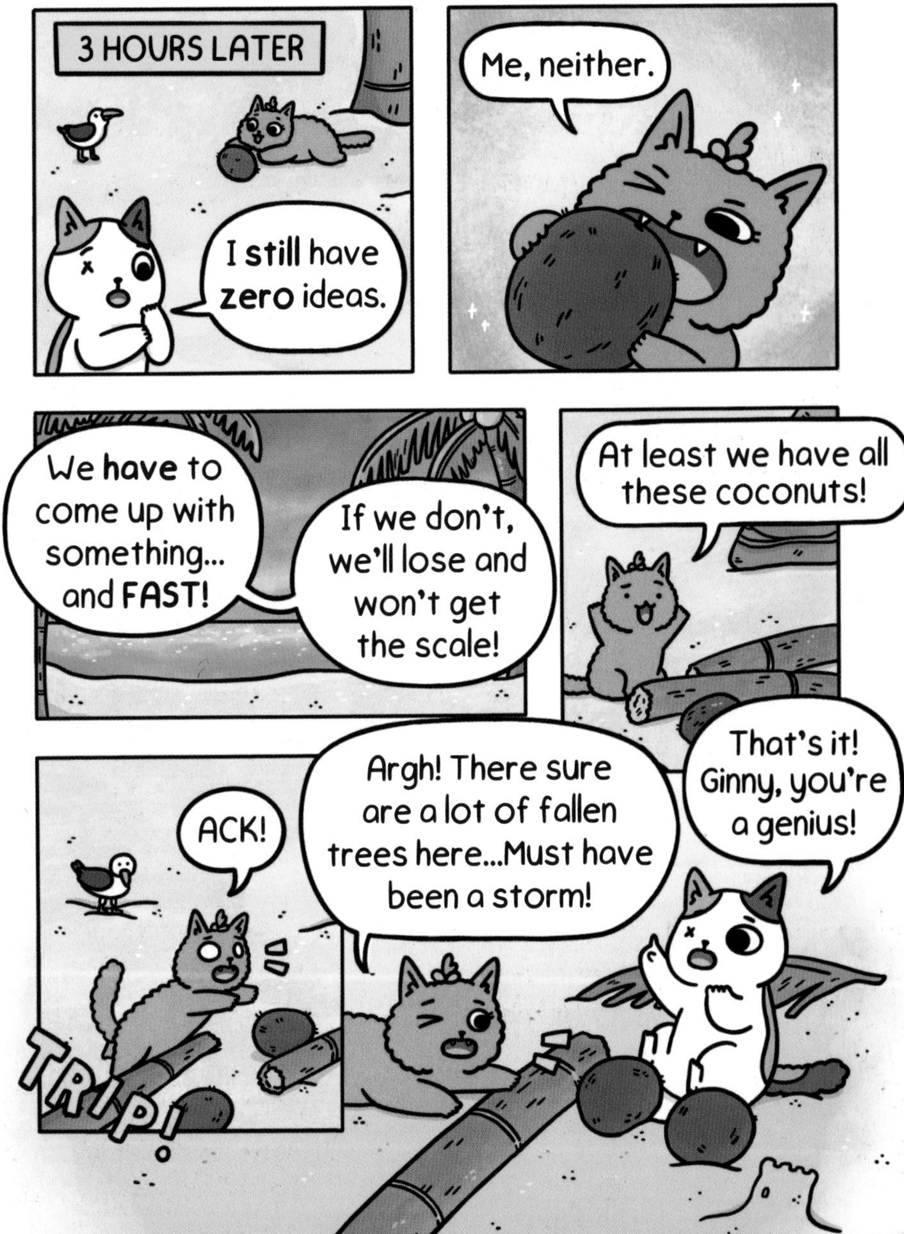
3 HOURS LATER
I still have zero ideas.
Me, neither.
We have to come up with something... and FAST!
If we don't, we'll lose and won't get the scale!
At least we have all these coconuts!
ACK!
TRIP!
Argh! There sure are a lot of fallen trees here...Must have been a storm!
That's it! Ginny, you're a genius!

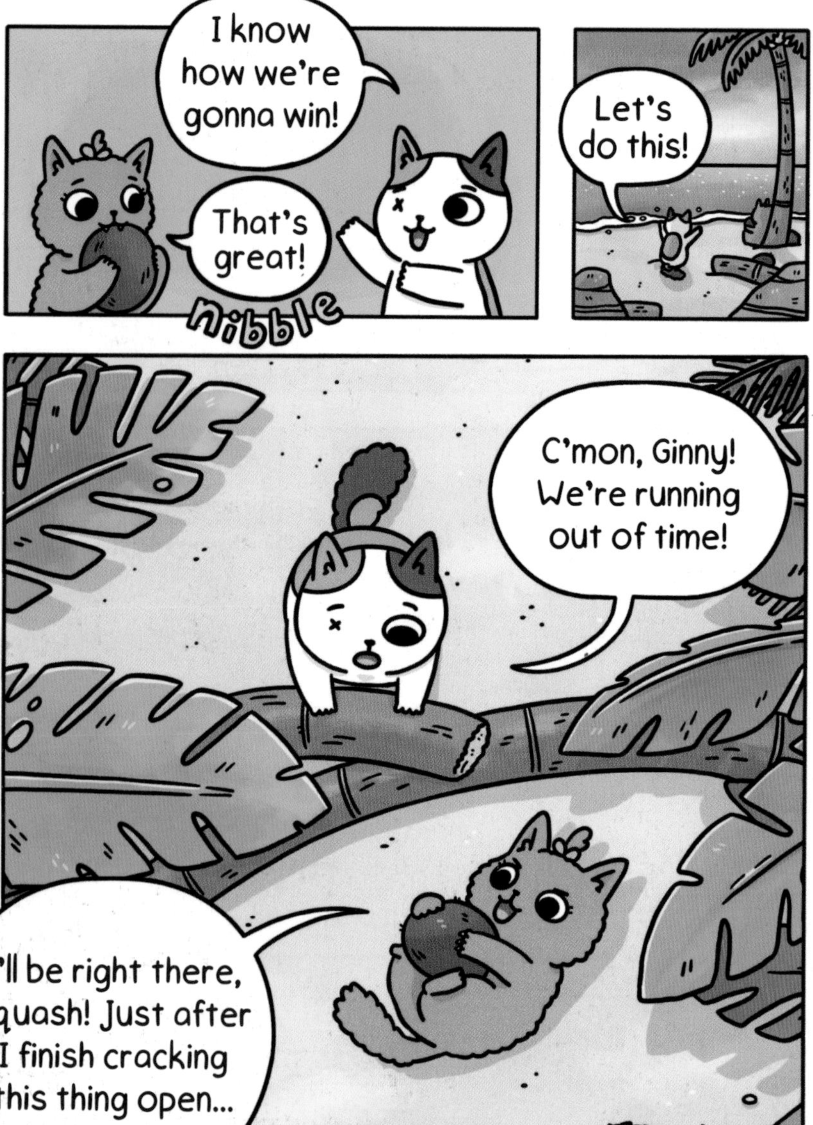

I know how we're gonna win!
That's great!
nibble
Let's do this!
C'mon, Ginny! We're running out of time!
I'll be right there, Squash! Just after I finish cracking this thing open...

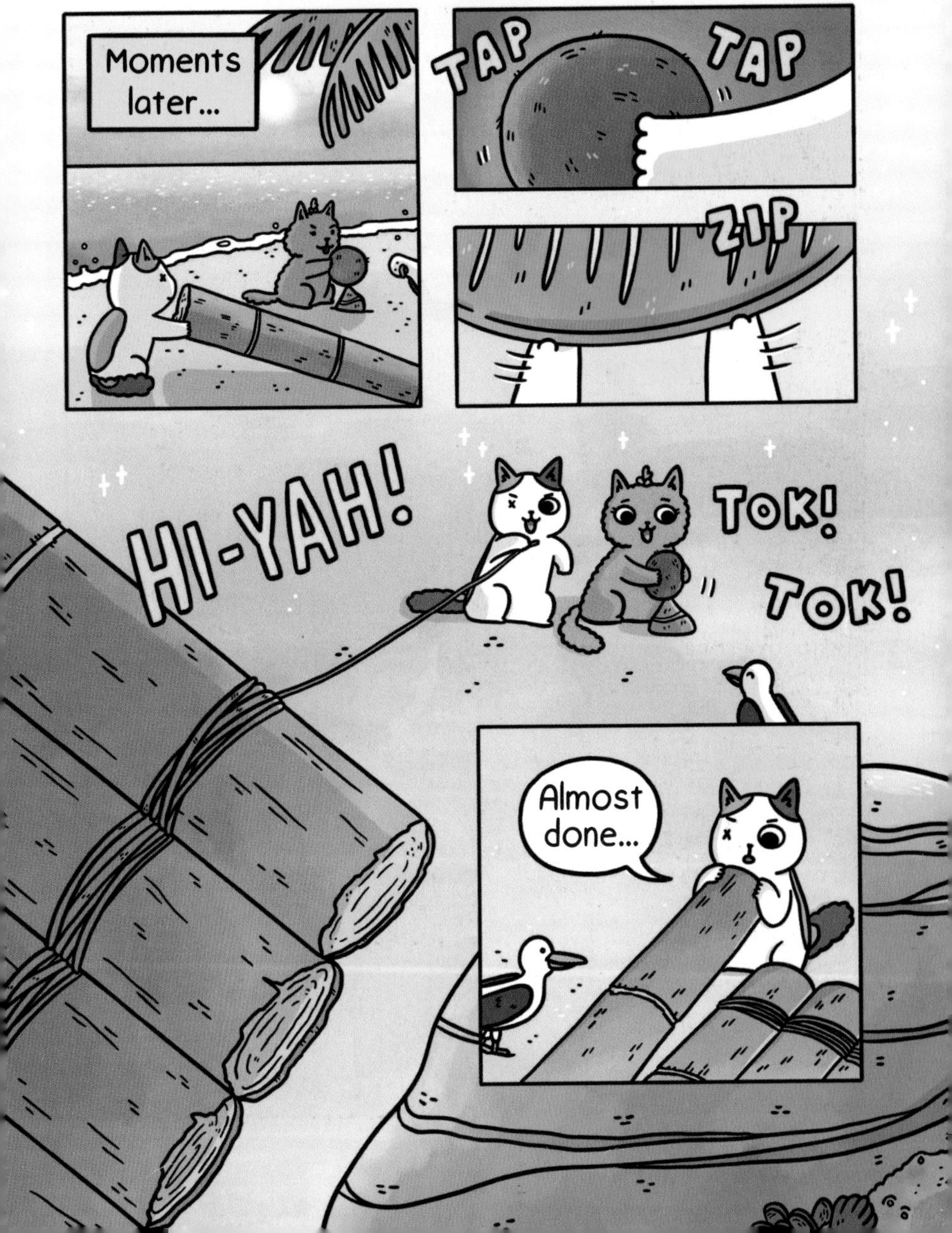
Moments later...
TAP TAP
ZIP
HI-YAH!
TOK! TOK!
Almost done...

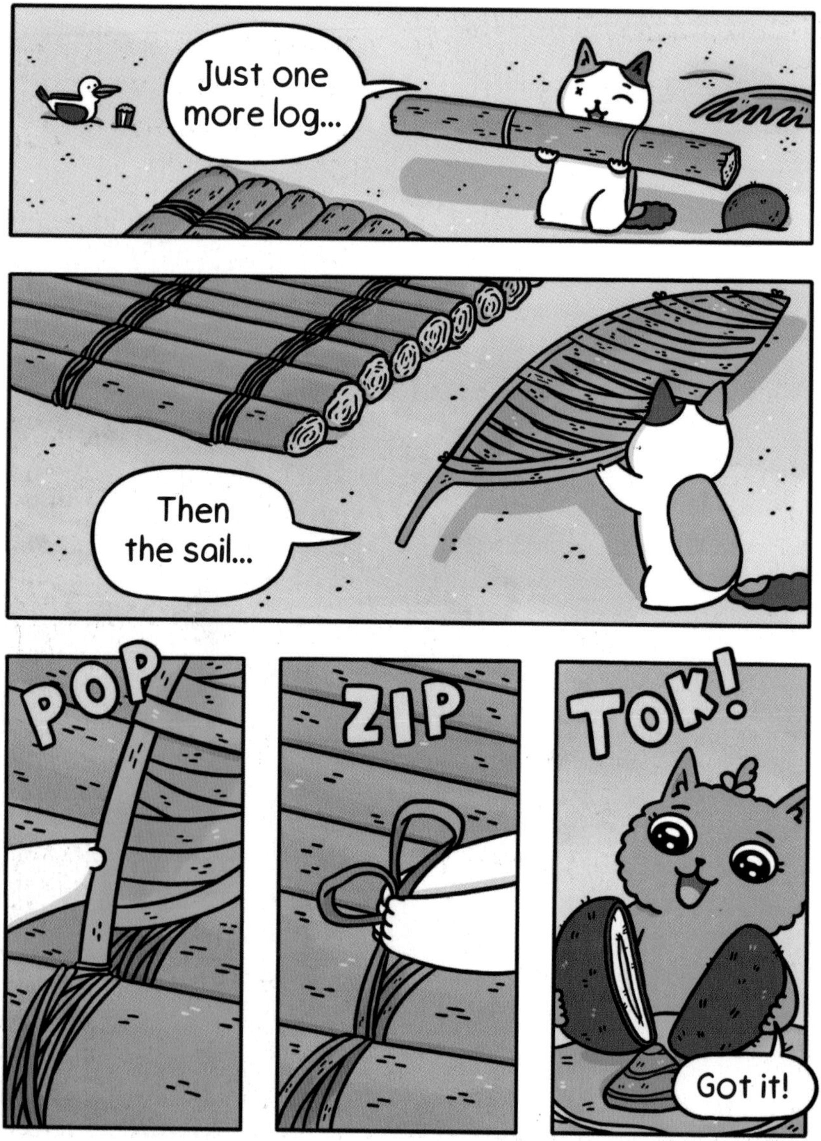
Just one more log...
Then the sail...
POP
ZIP
TOK!
Got it!

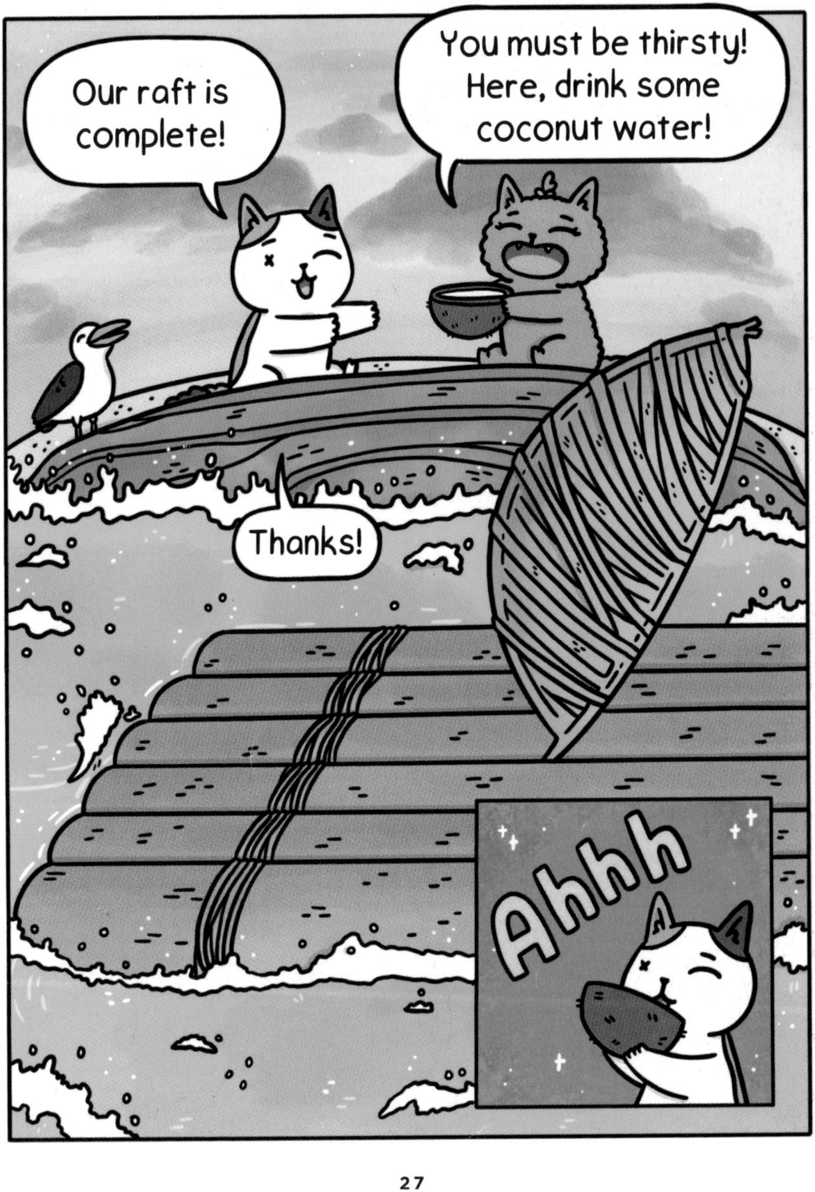
Our raft is complete!
You must be thirsty! Here, drink some coconut water!
Thanks!
Ahhh

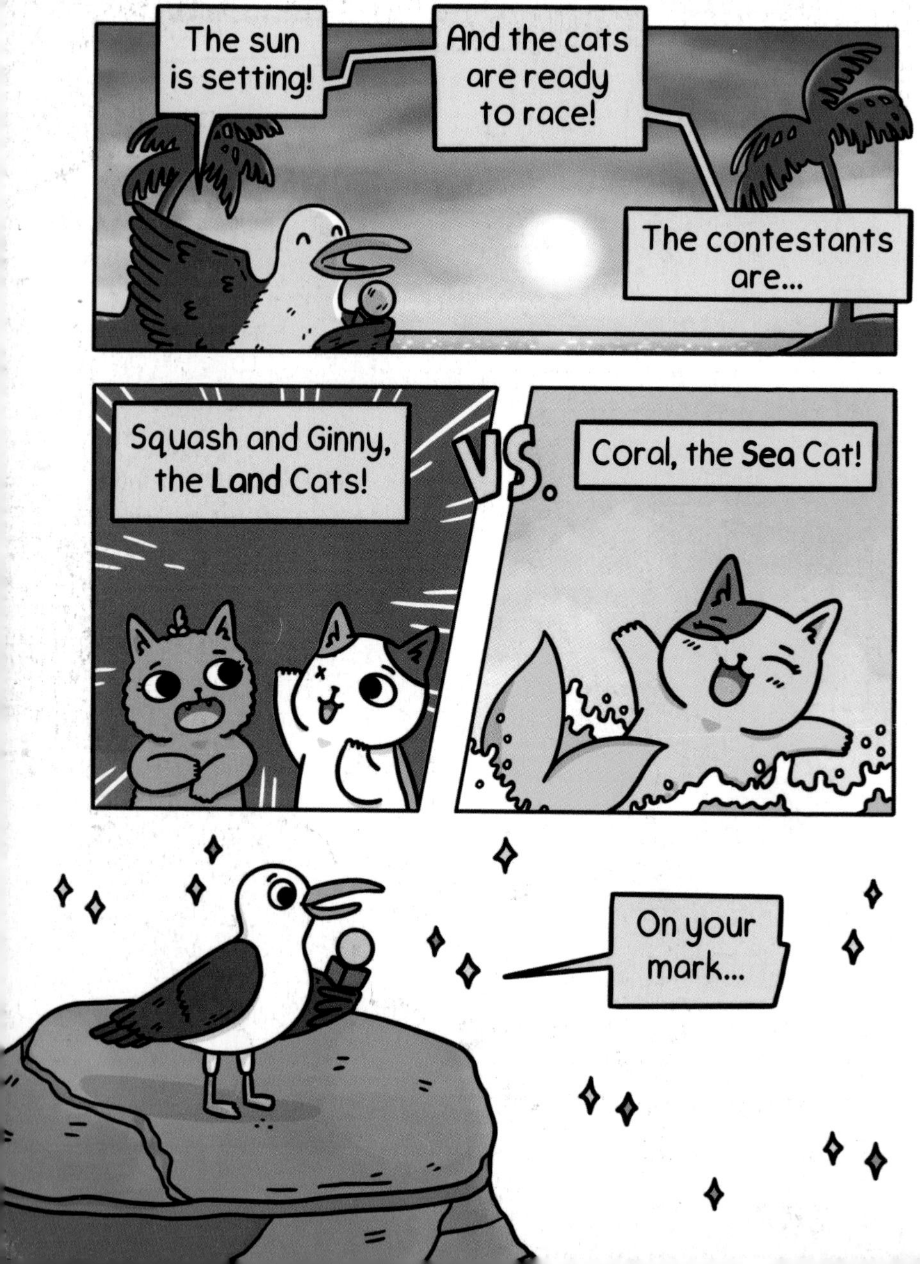

The sun is setting!
And the cats are ready to race!
The contestants are...
Squash and Ginny, the Land Cats!
VS.
Coral, the Sea Cat!
On your mark...

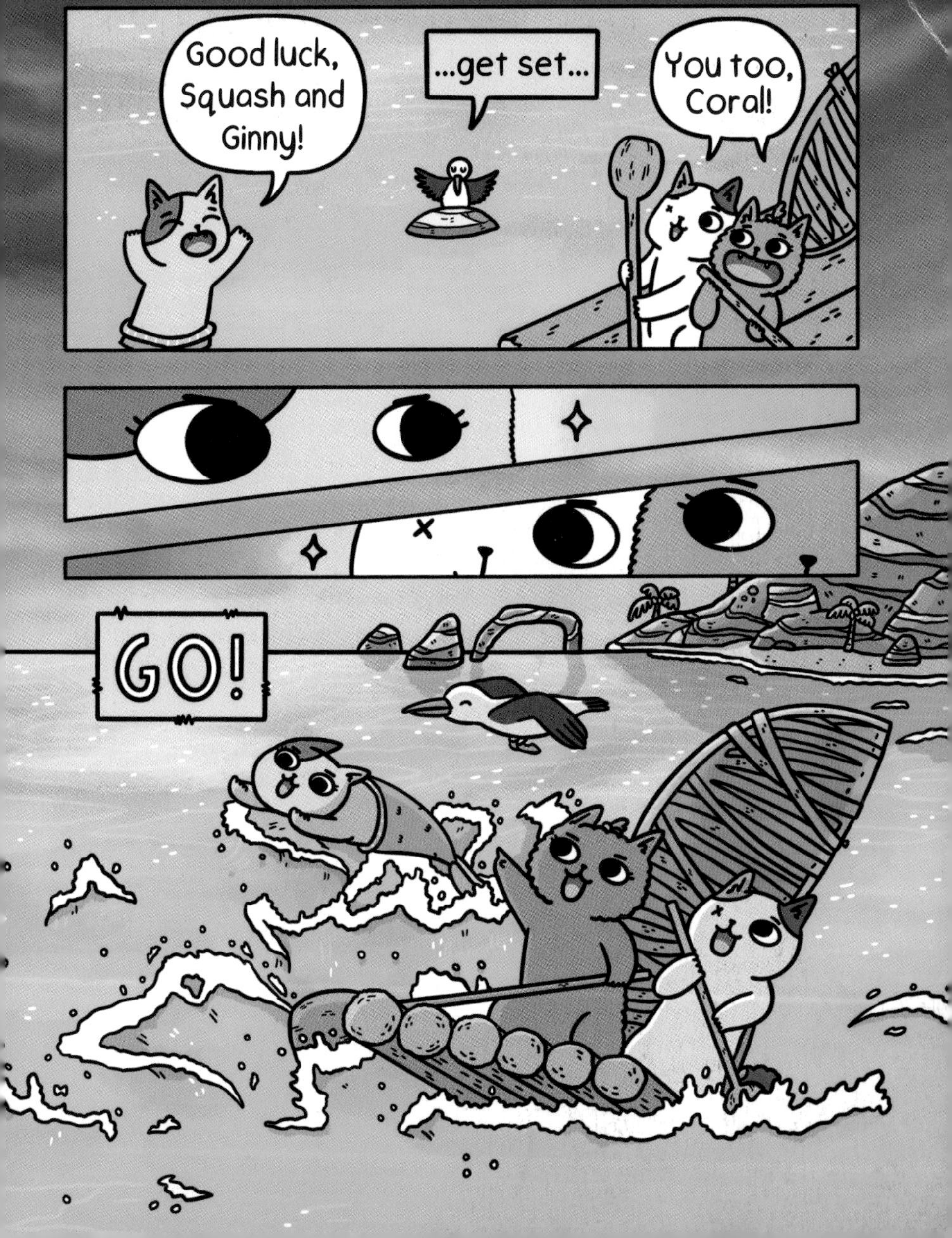
Good luck, Squash and Ginny!
...get set...
You too, Coral!
GO!

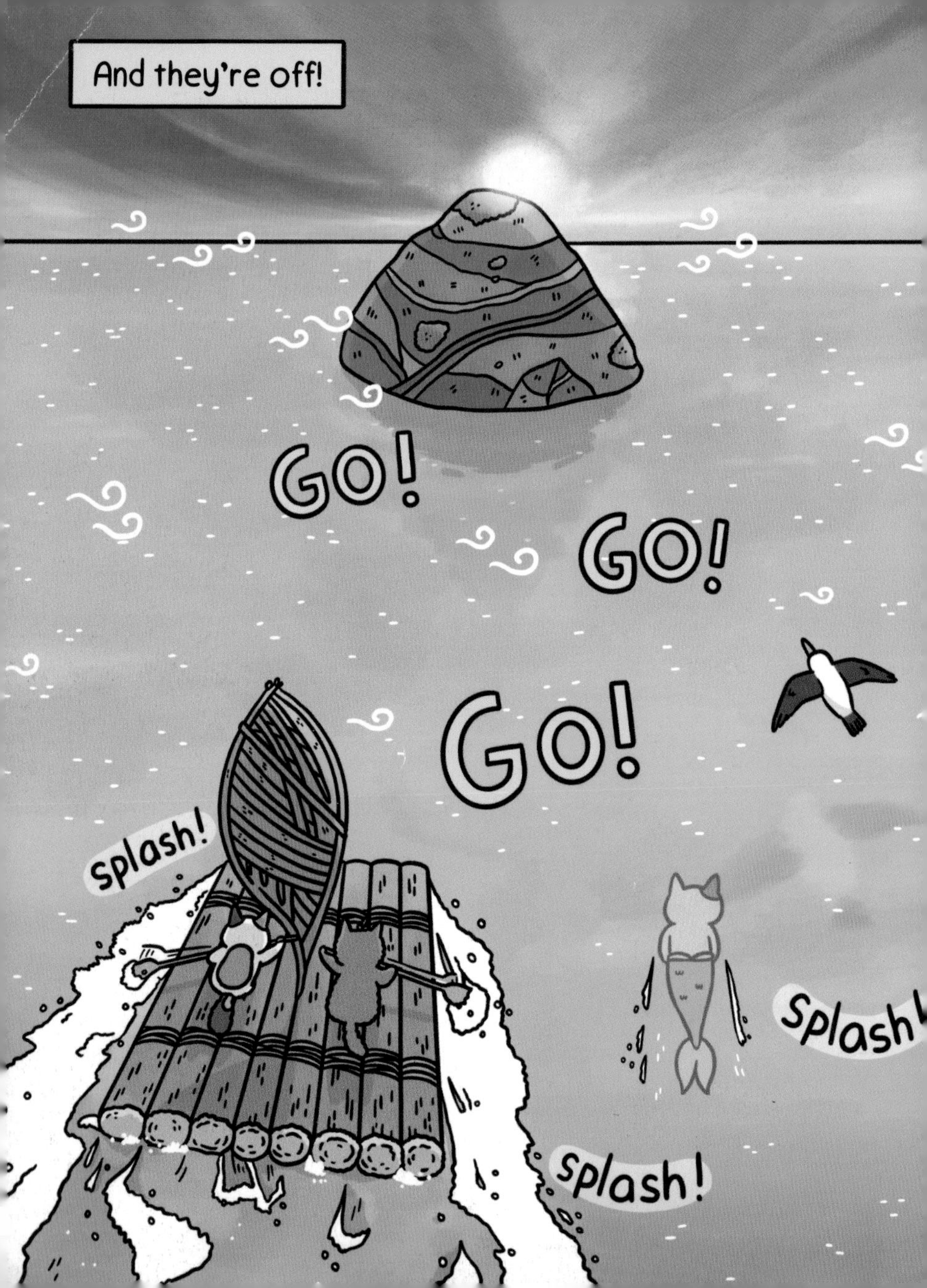

And they're off!
GO!
GO!
GO!
splash!
Splash!
splash!

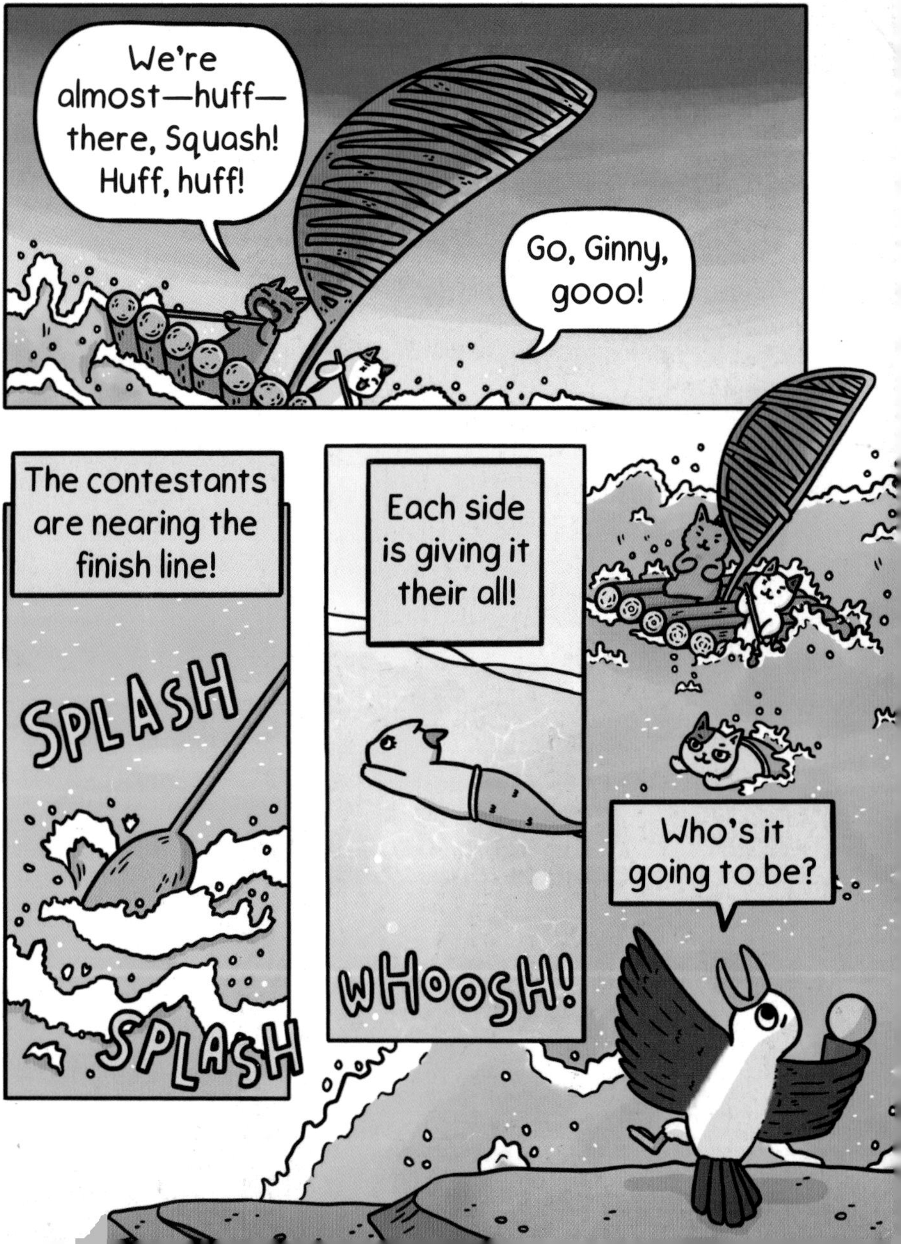
We're almost—huff—there, Squash! Huff, huff!
Go, Ginny, gooo!
The contestants are nearing the finish line!
SPLASH
SPLASH
Each side is giving it their all!
WHOOSH!
Who's it going to be?

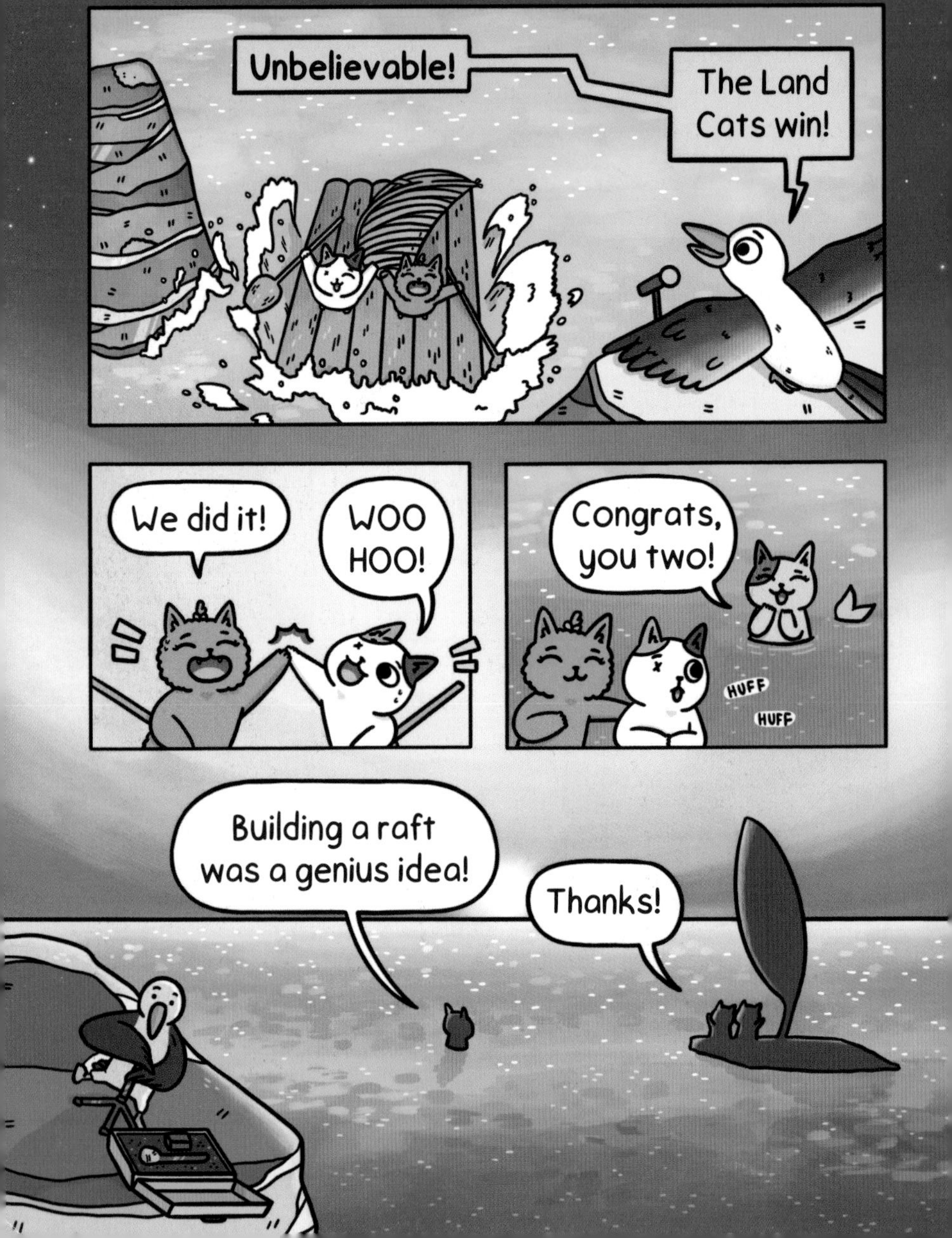
Unbelievable!
The Land Cats win!
We did it!
WOO HOO!
Congrats, you two!
HUFF
HUFF
Building a raft was a genius idea!
Thanks!

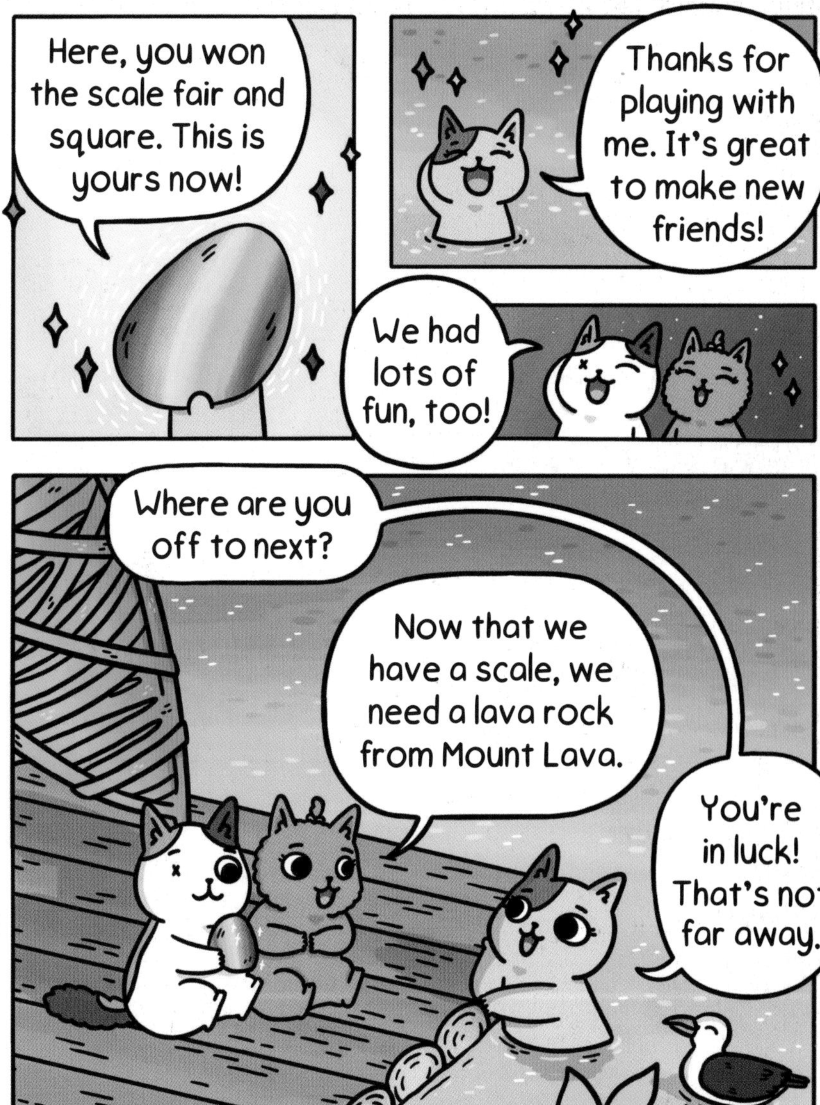
Here, you won the scale fair and square. This is yours now!
Thanks for playing with me. It's great to make new friends!
We had lots of fun, too!
Where are you off to next?
Now that we have a scale, we need a lava rock from Mount Lava.
You're in luck! That's not far away.

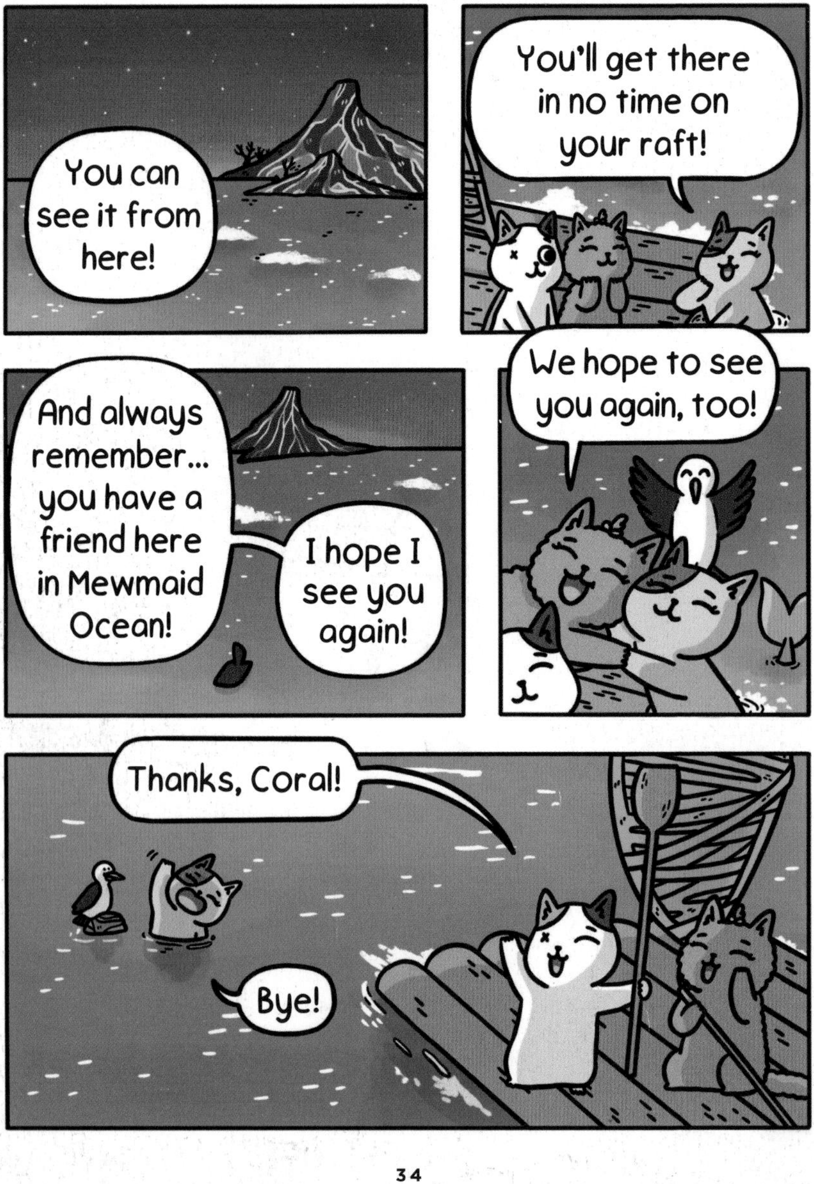
You can see it from here!
You'll get there in no time on your raft!
And always remember... you have a friend here in Mewmaid Ocean!
I hope I see you again!
We hope to see you again, too!
Thanks, Coral!
Bye!

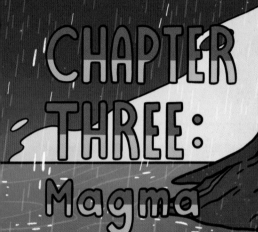

CHAPTER THREE:
Magma

We're here!

Finally! Maybe we'll find some snacks...I'm hungry.

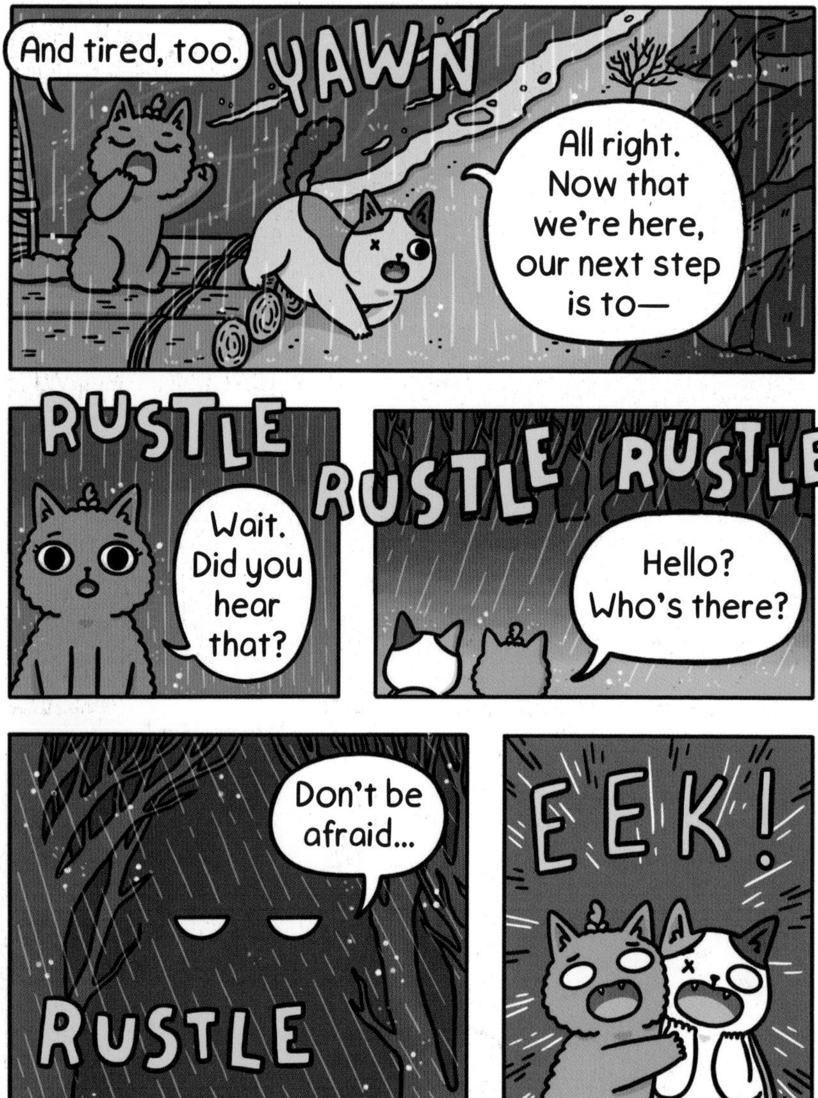
And tired, too.
YAWN
All right. Now that we're here, our next step is to—
RUSTLE
Wait. Did you hear that?
RUSTLE RUSTLE
Hello? Who's there?
Don't be afraid...
RUSTLE
EEK!

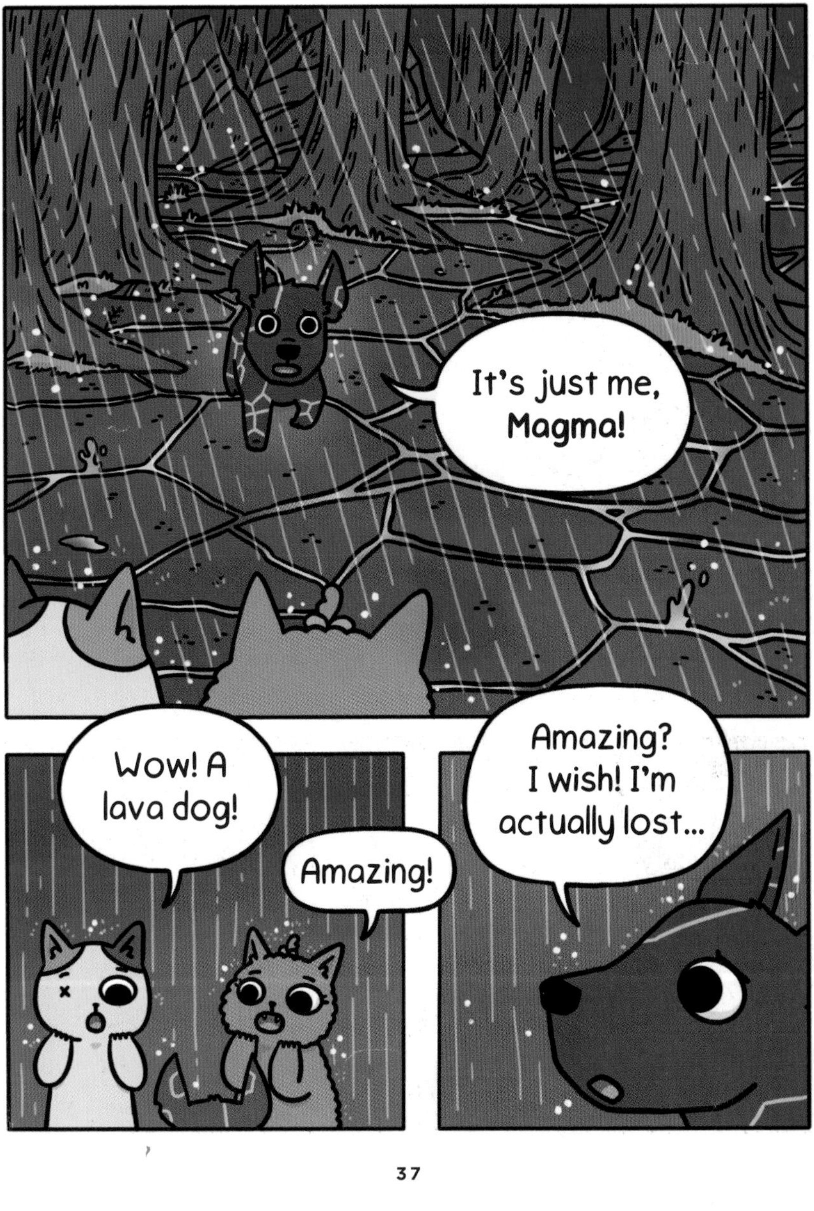
It's just me, Magma!
Wow! A lava dog!
Amazing!
Amazing? I wish! I'm actually lost...

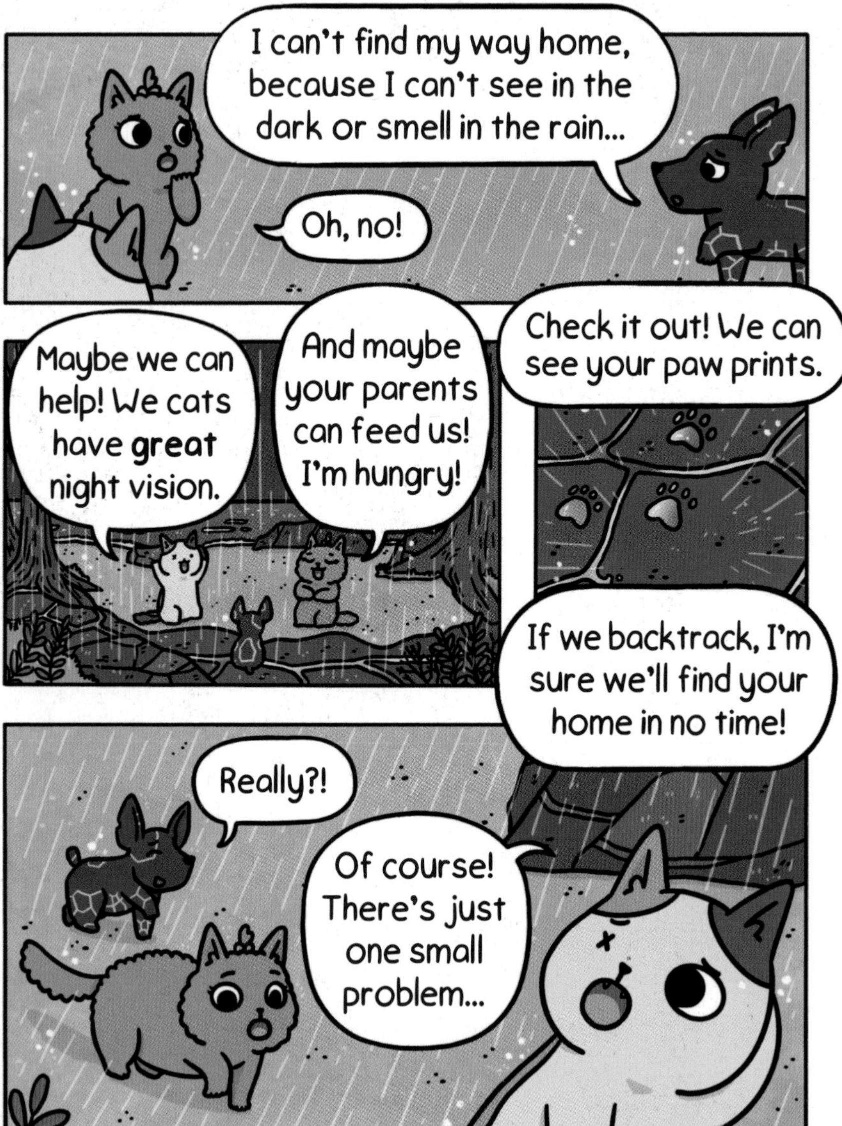
I can't find my way home, because I can't see in the dark or smell in the rain...
Oh, no!
Maybe we can help! We cats have **great** night vision.
And maybe your parents can feed us! I'm hungry!
Check it out! We can see your paw prints.
If we backtrack, I'm sure we'll find your home in no time!
Really?!
Of course! There's just one small problem...

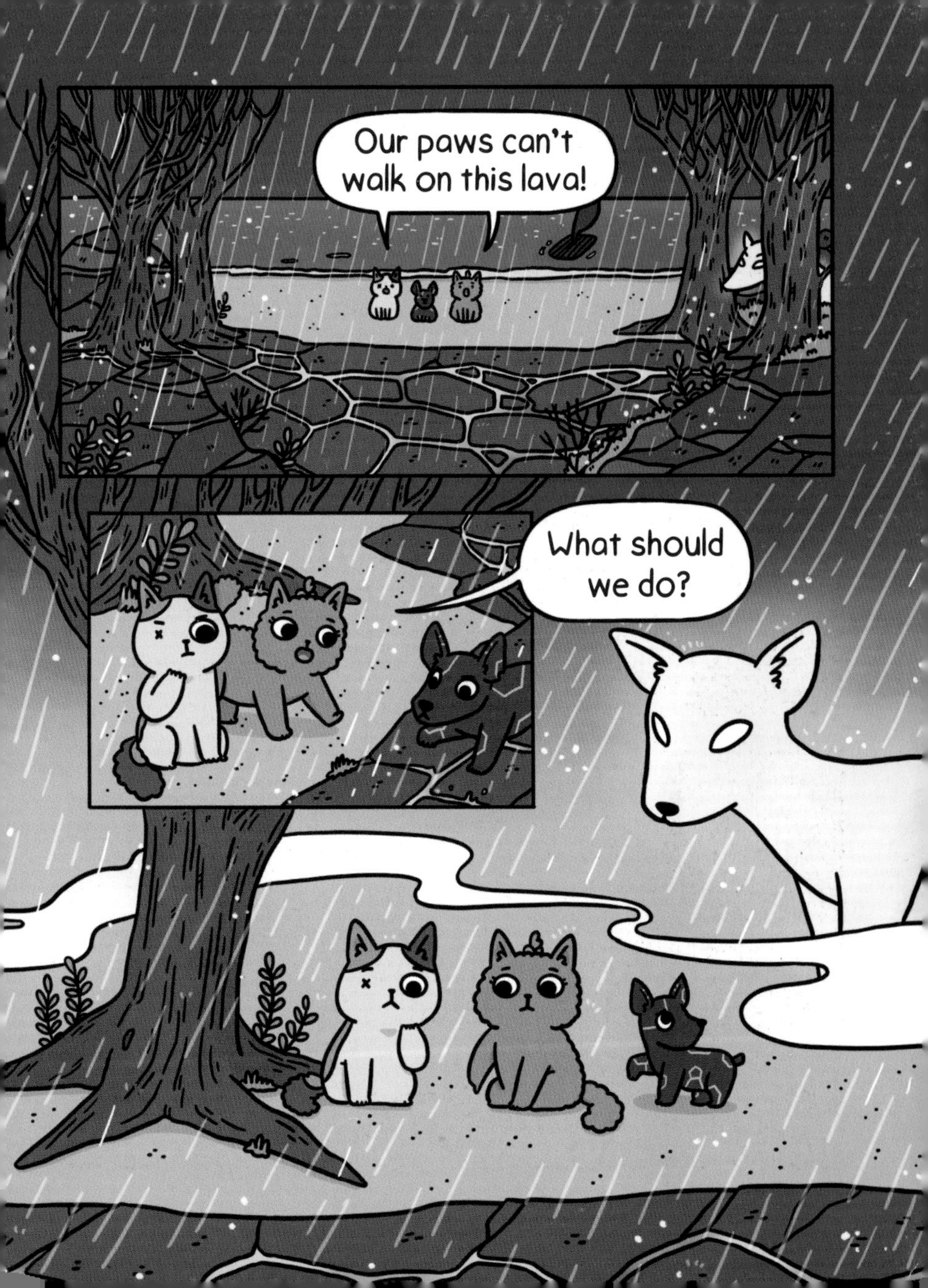
Our paws can't walk on this lava!
What should we do?

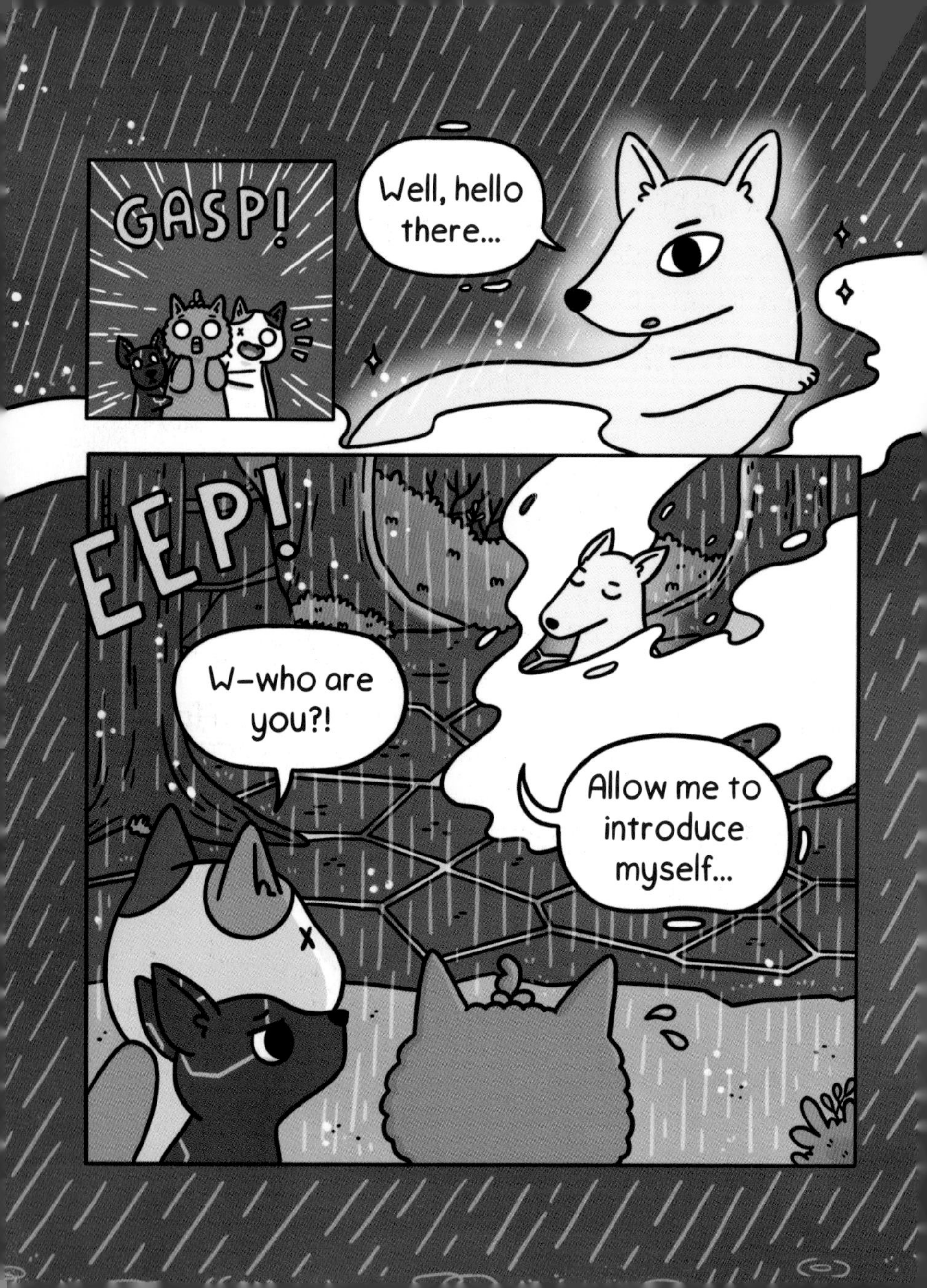
GASP!
Well, hello there...
EEP!
W-who are you?!
Allow me to introduce myself...

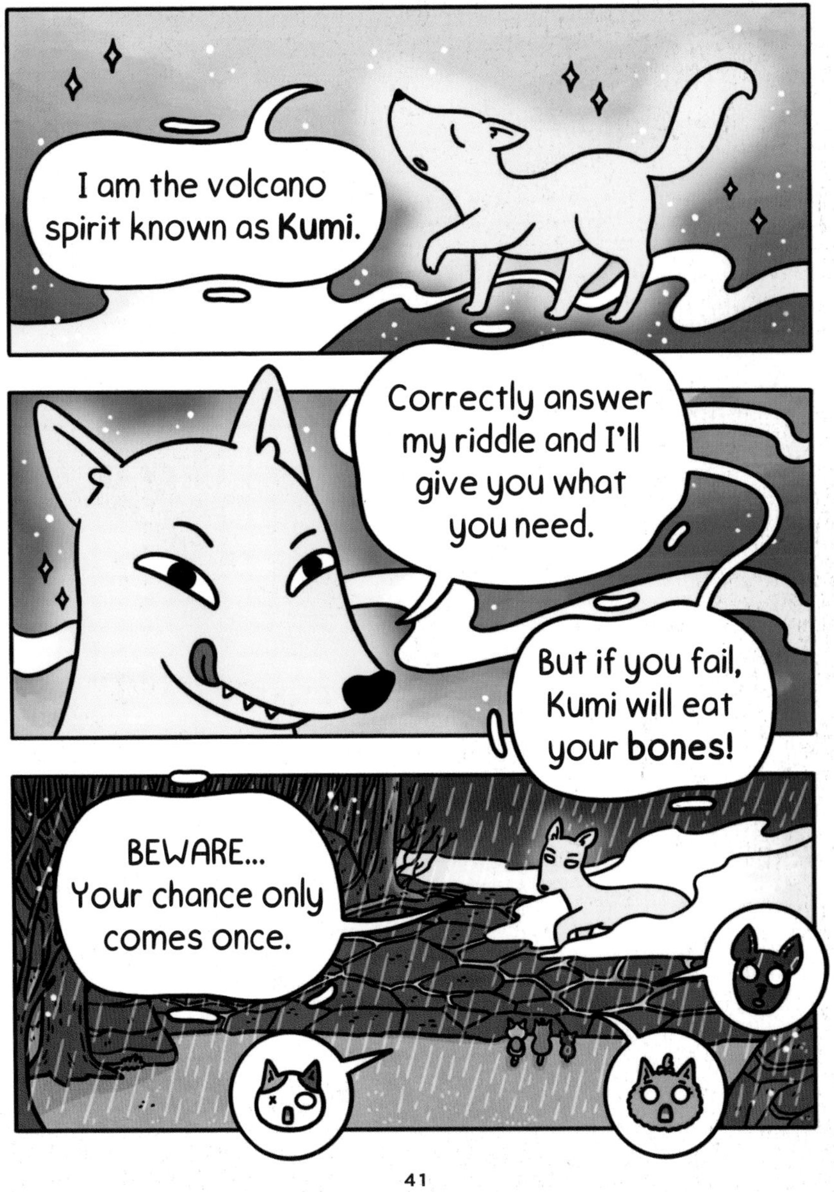
I am the volcano spirit known as **Kumi**.
Correctly answer my riddle and I'll give you what you need.
But if you fail, Kumi will eat your **bones**!
BEWARE... Your chance only comes once.

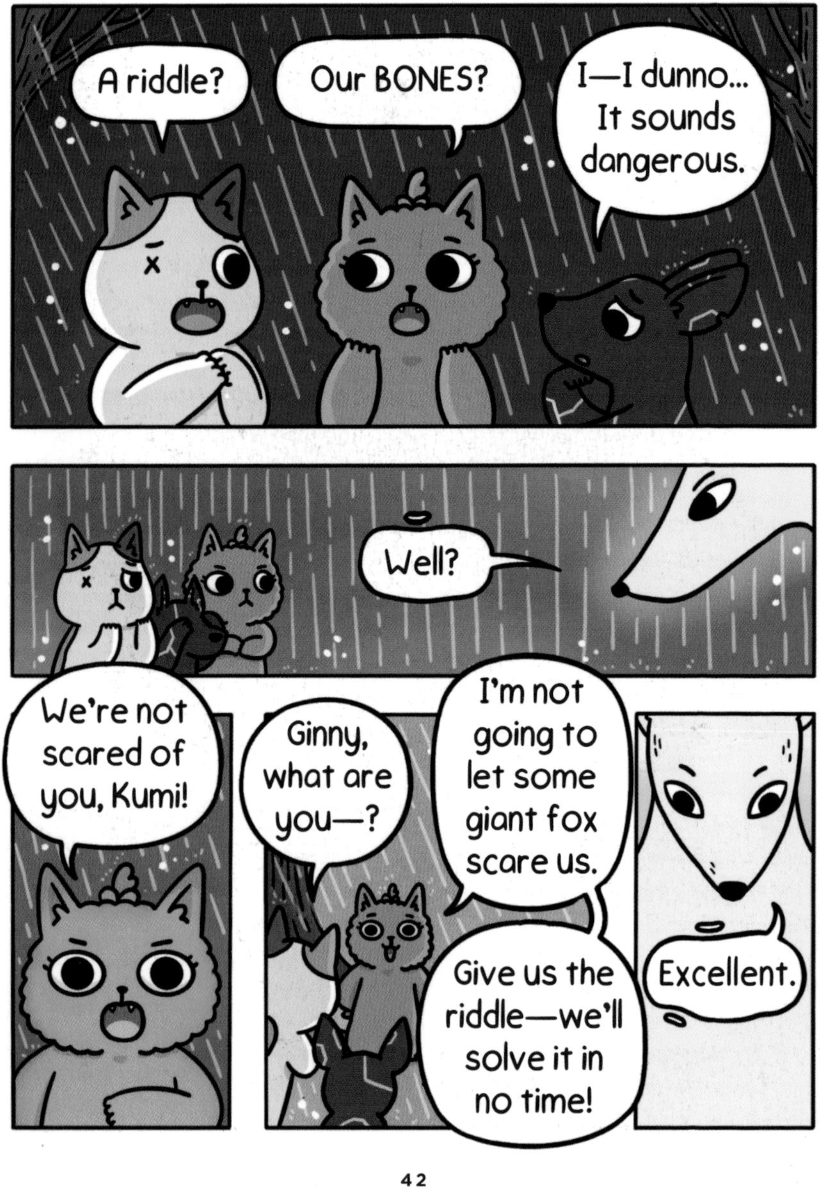
A riddle?
Our BONES?
I—I dunno... It sounds dangerous.
Well?
We're not scared of you, Kumi!
Ginny, what are you—?
I'm not going to let some giant fox scare us.
Give us the riddle—we'll solve it in no time!
Excellent.

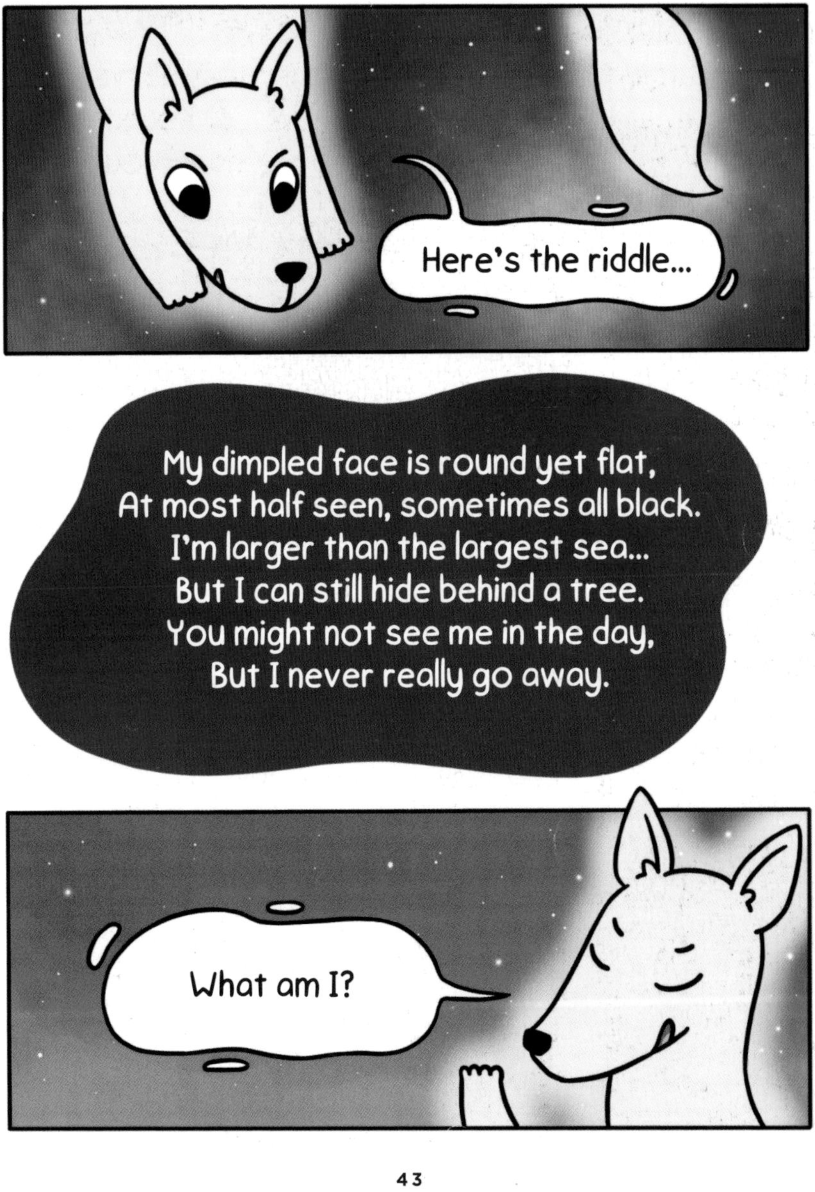
Here's the riddle...
My dimpled face is round yet flat,
At most half seen, sometimes all black.
I'm larger than the largest sea...
But I can still hide behind a tree.
You might not see me in the day,
But I never really go away.
What am I?

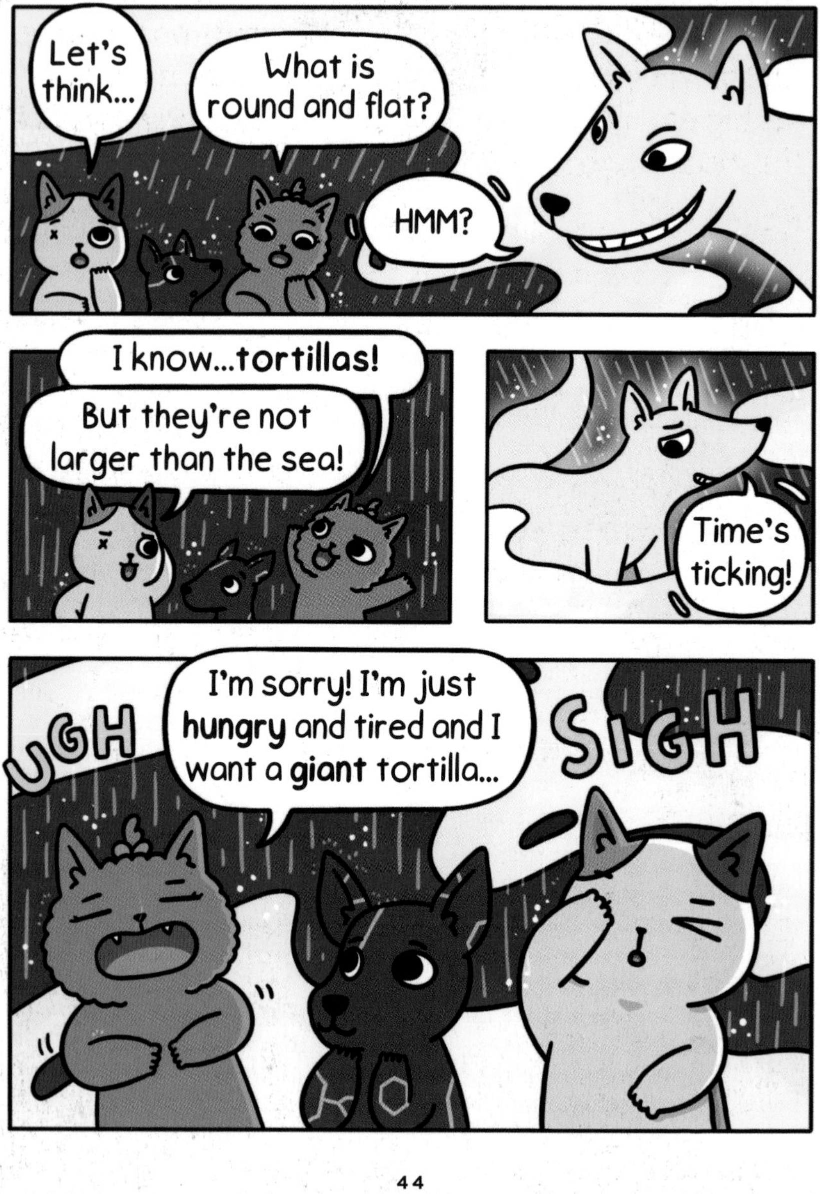
Let's think...
What is round and flat?
HMM?
I know...tortillas!
But they're not larger than the sea!
Time's ticking!
UGH
I'm sorry! I'm just hungry and tired and I want a giant tortilla...
SIGH

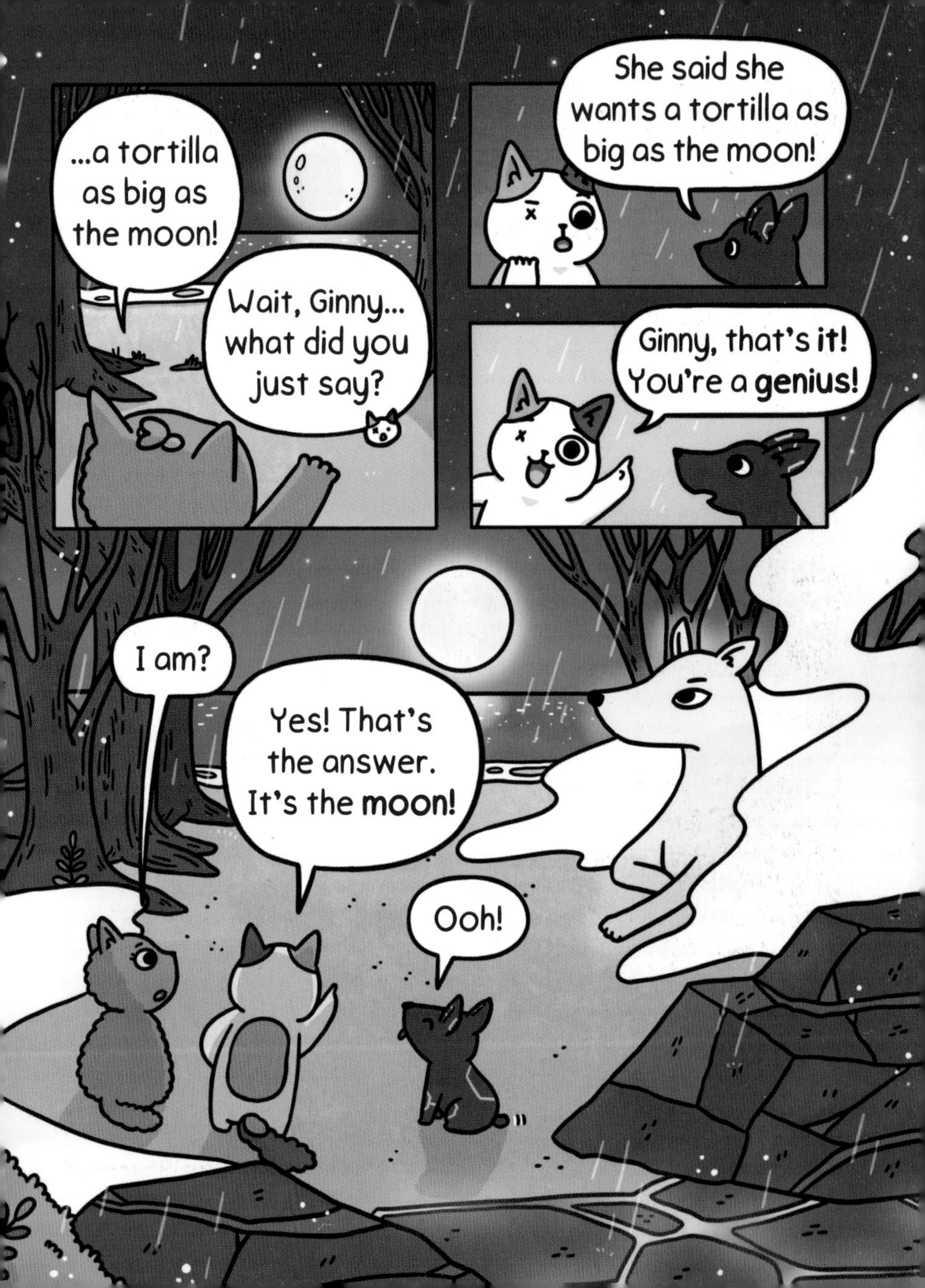
...a tortilla as big as the moon!
Wait, Ginny... what did you just say?
She said she wants a tortilla as big as the moon!
Ginny, that's **it**! You're a **genius**!
I am?
Yes! That's the answer. It's the **moon**!
Ooh!

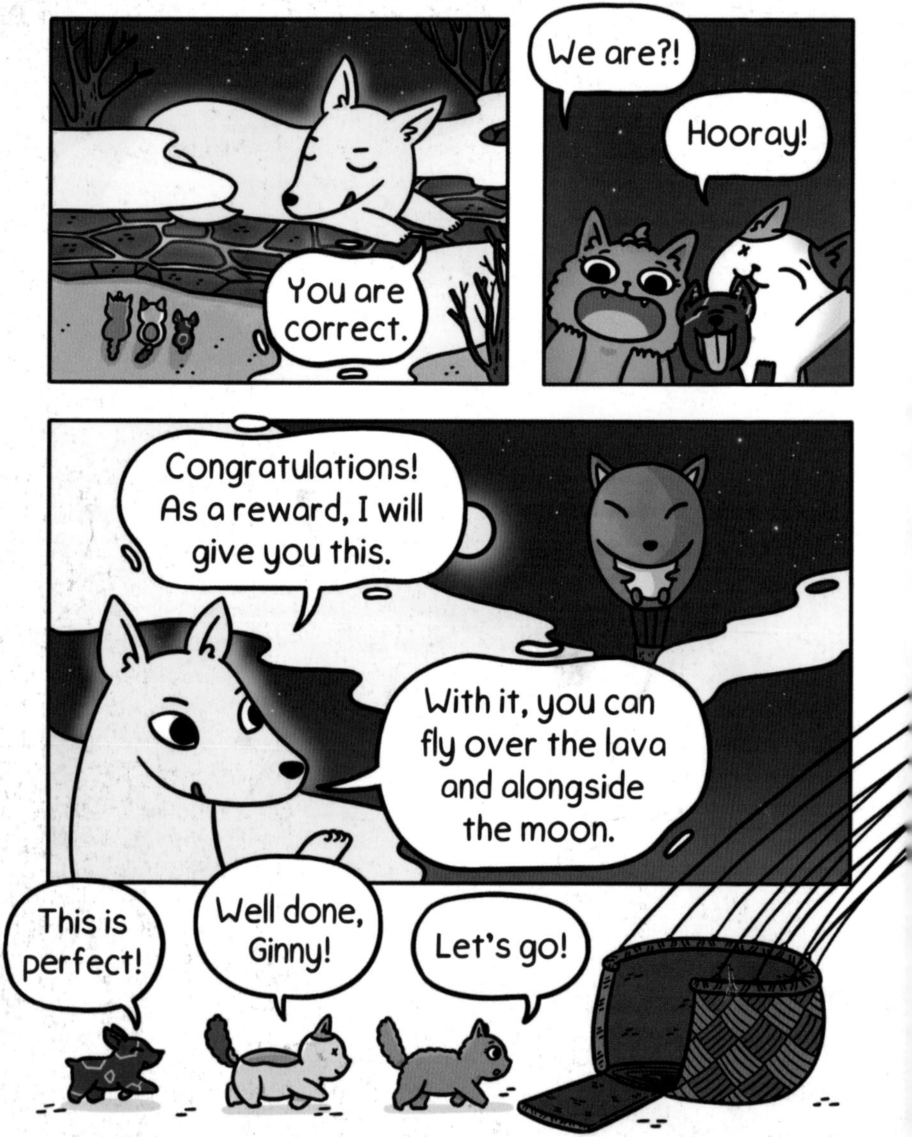
You are correct.
We are?!
Hooray!
Congratulations! As a reward, I will give you this.
With it, you can fly over the lava and alongside the moon.
This is perfect!
Well done, Ginny!
Let's go!

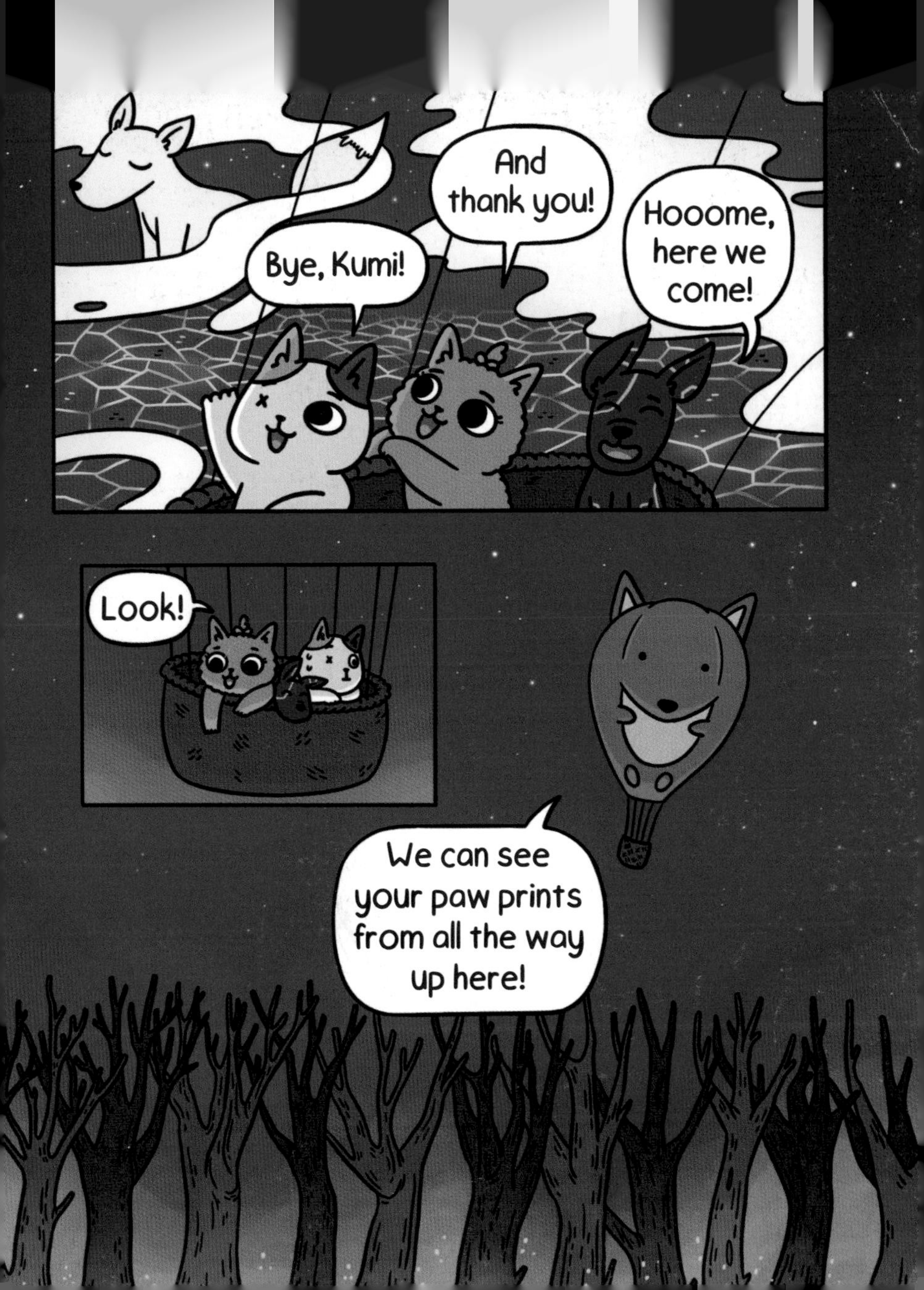
Bye, Kumi!
And thank you!
Hooome, here we come!
Look!
We can see your paw prints from all the way up here!

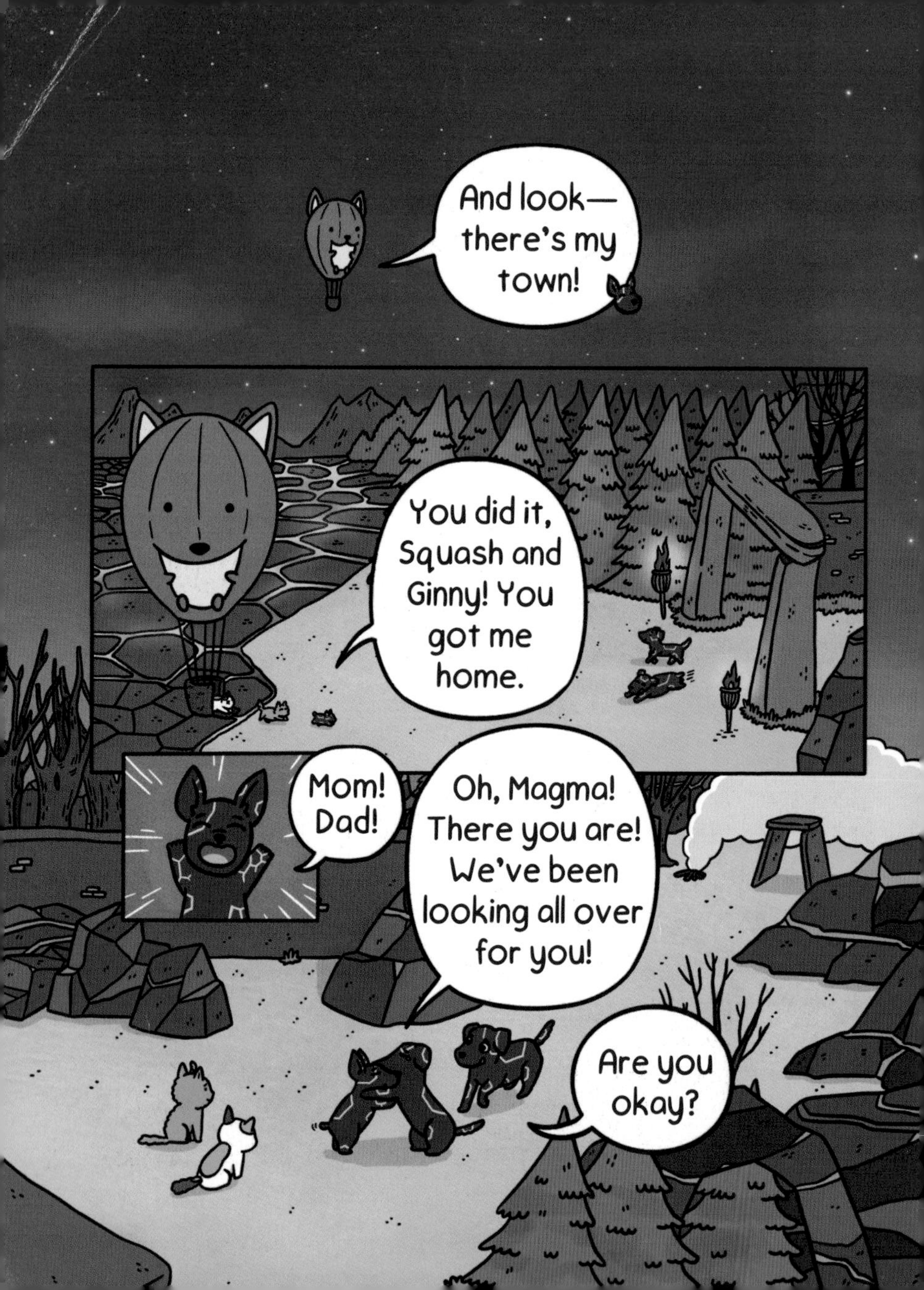
And look—there's my town!
You did it, Squash and Ginny! You got me home.
Mom! Dad!
Oh, Magma! There you are! We've been looking all over for you!
Are you okay?

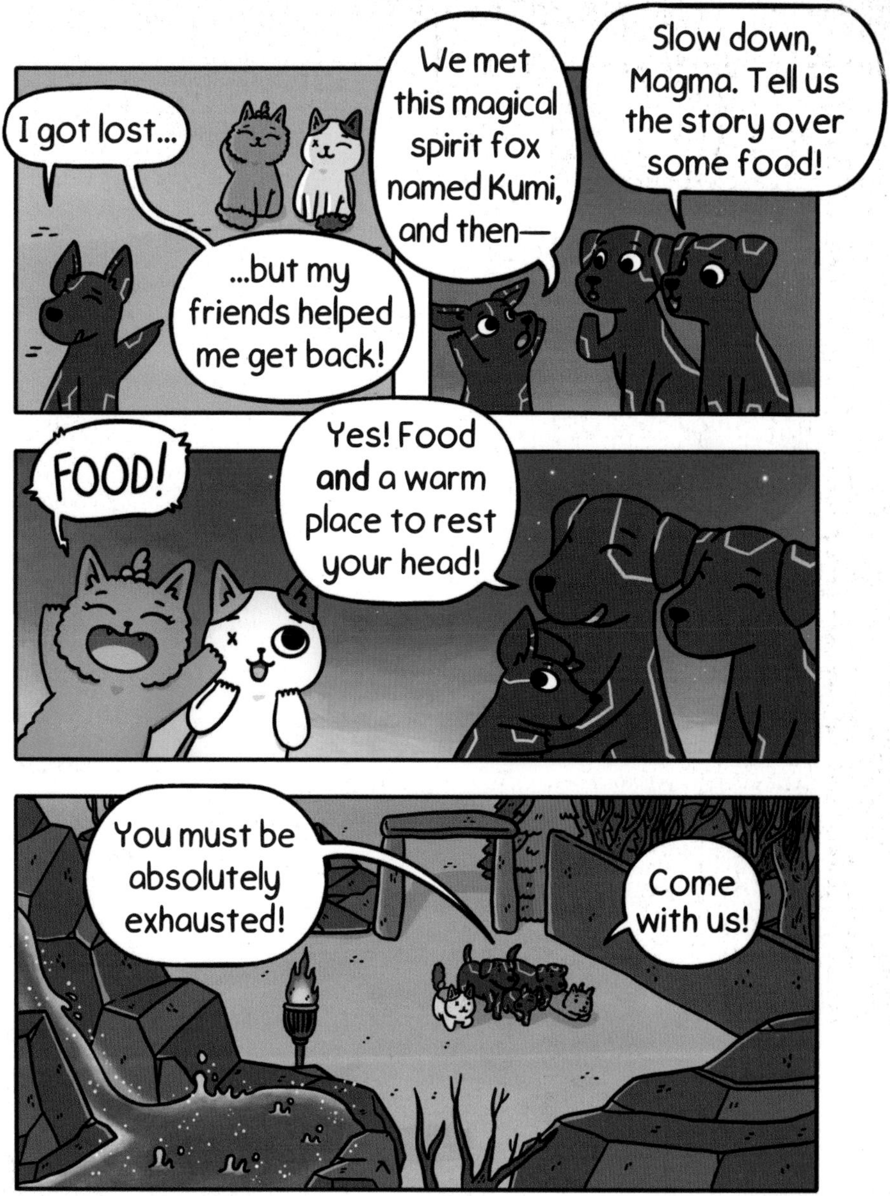
I got lost...
...but my friends helped me get back!
We met this magical spirit fox named Kumi, and then—
Slow down, Magma. Tell us the story over some food!
FOOD!
Yes! Food and a warm place to rest your head!
You must be absolutely exhausted!
Come with us!

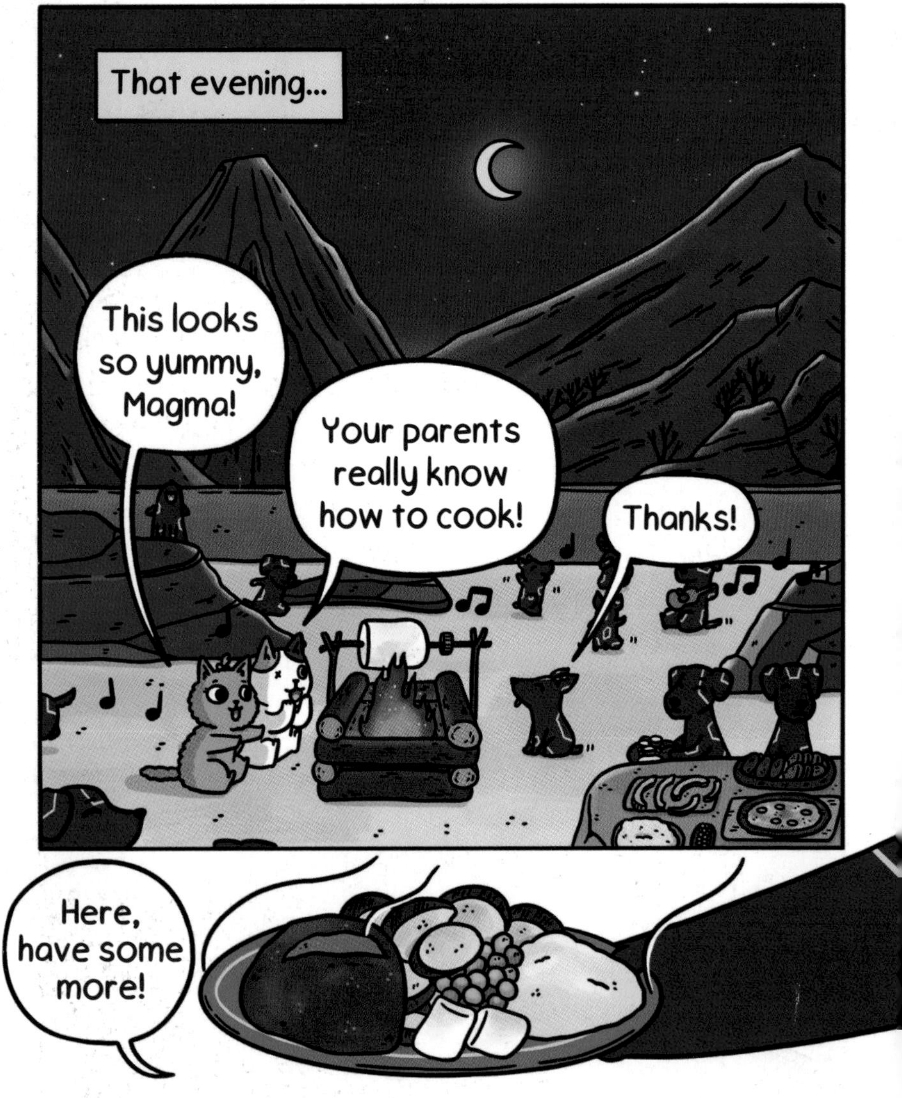
That evening...
This looks so yummy, Magma!
Your parents really know how to cook!
Thanks!
Here, have some more!

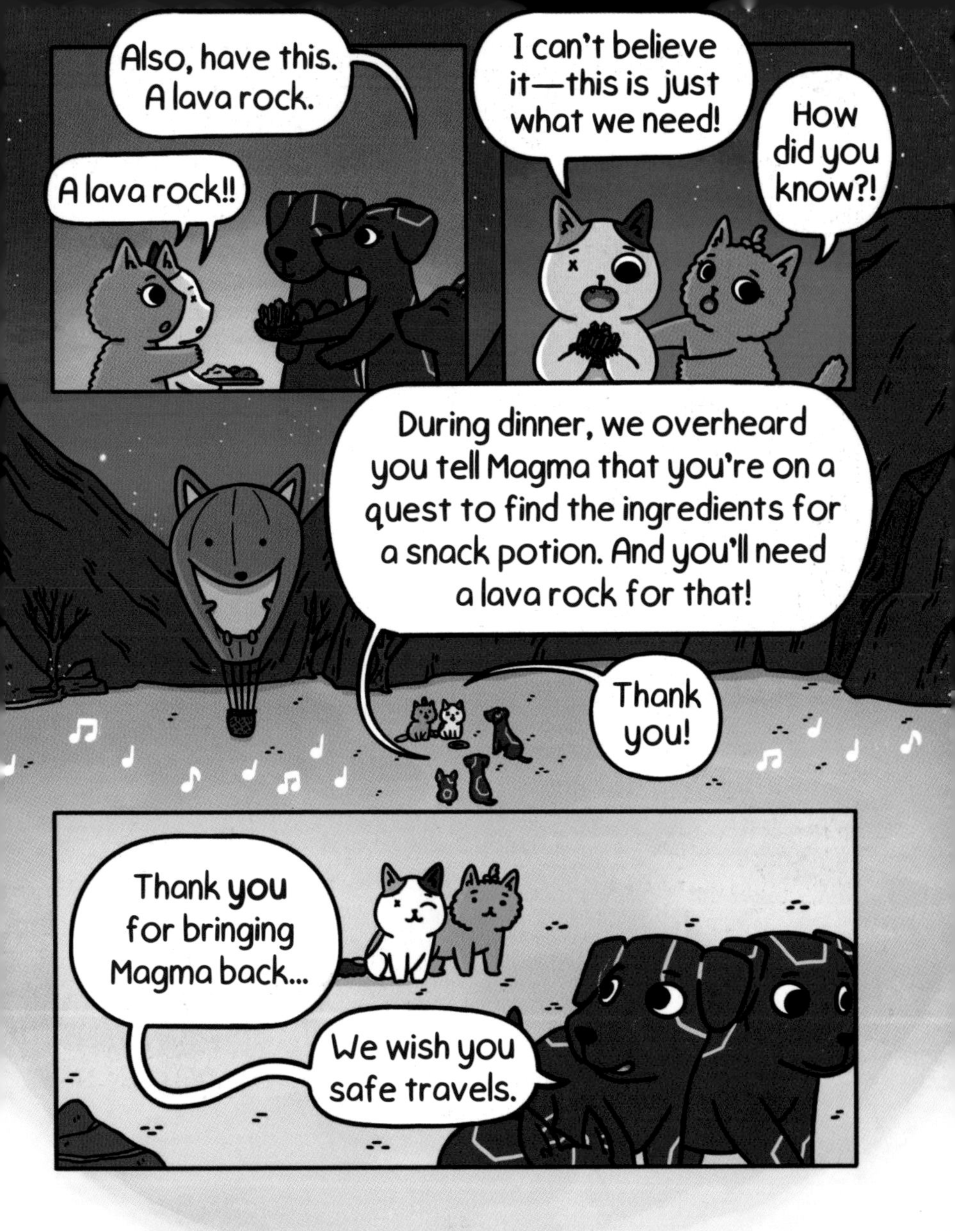
Also, have this. A lava rock.
A lava rock!!
I can't believe it—this is just what we need!
How did you know?!
During dinner, we overheard you tell Magma that you're on a quest to find the ingredients for a snack potion. And you'll need a lava rock for that!
Thank you!
Thank you for bringing Magma back...
We wish you safe travels.

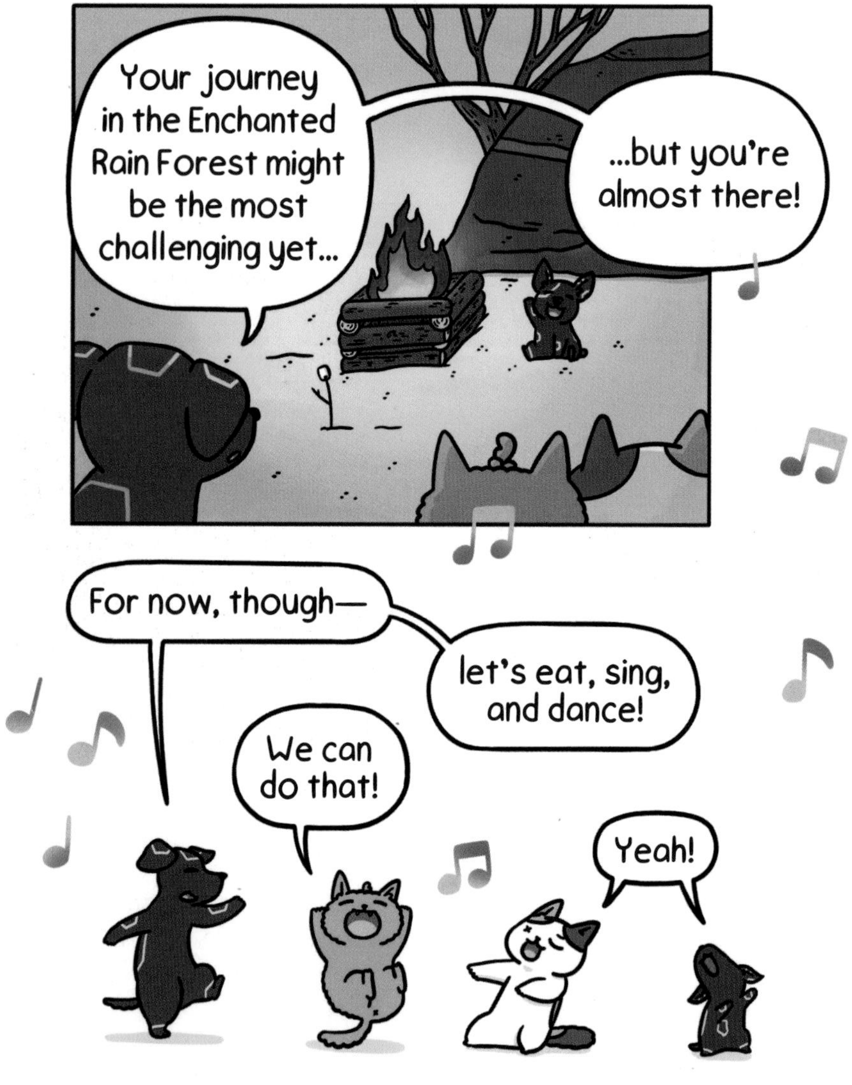
Your journey in the Enchanted Rain Forest might be the most challenging yet...
...but you're almost there!
For now, though—
let's eat, sing, and dance!
We can do that!
Yeah!

CHAPTER FOUR: Lotus

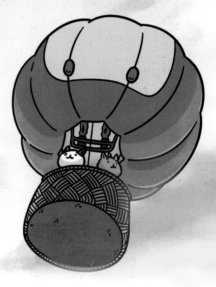

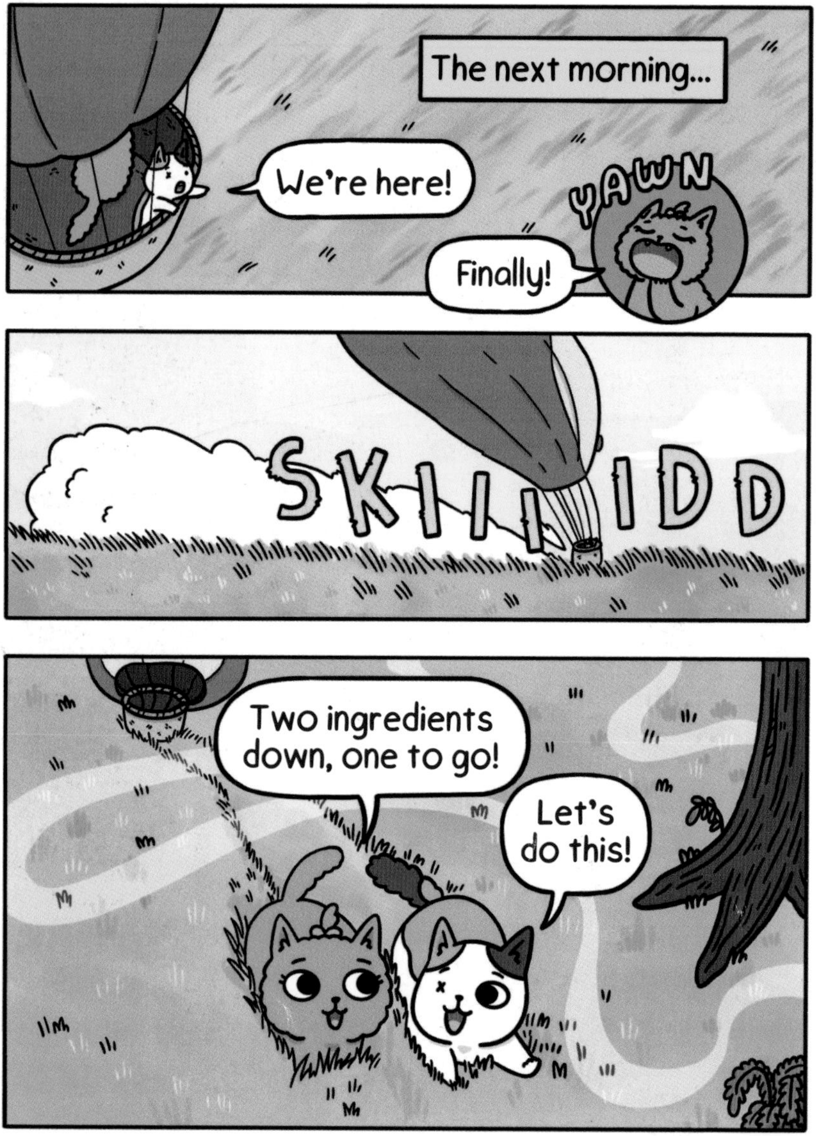
The next morning...
We're here!
YAWN
Finally!
SKIIIIDD
Two ingredients down, one to go!
Let's do this!

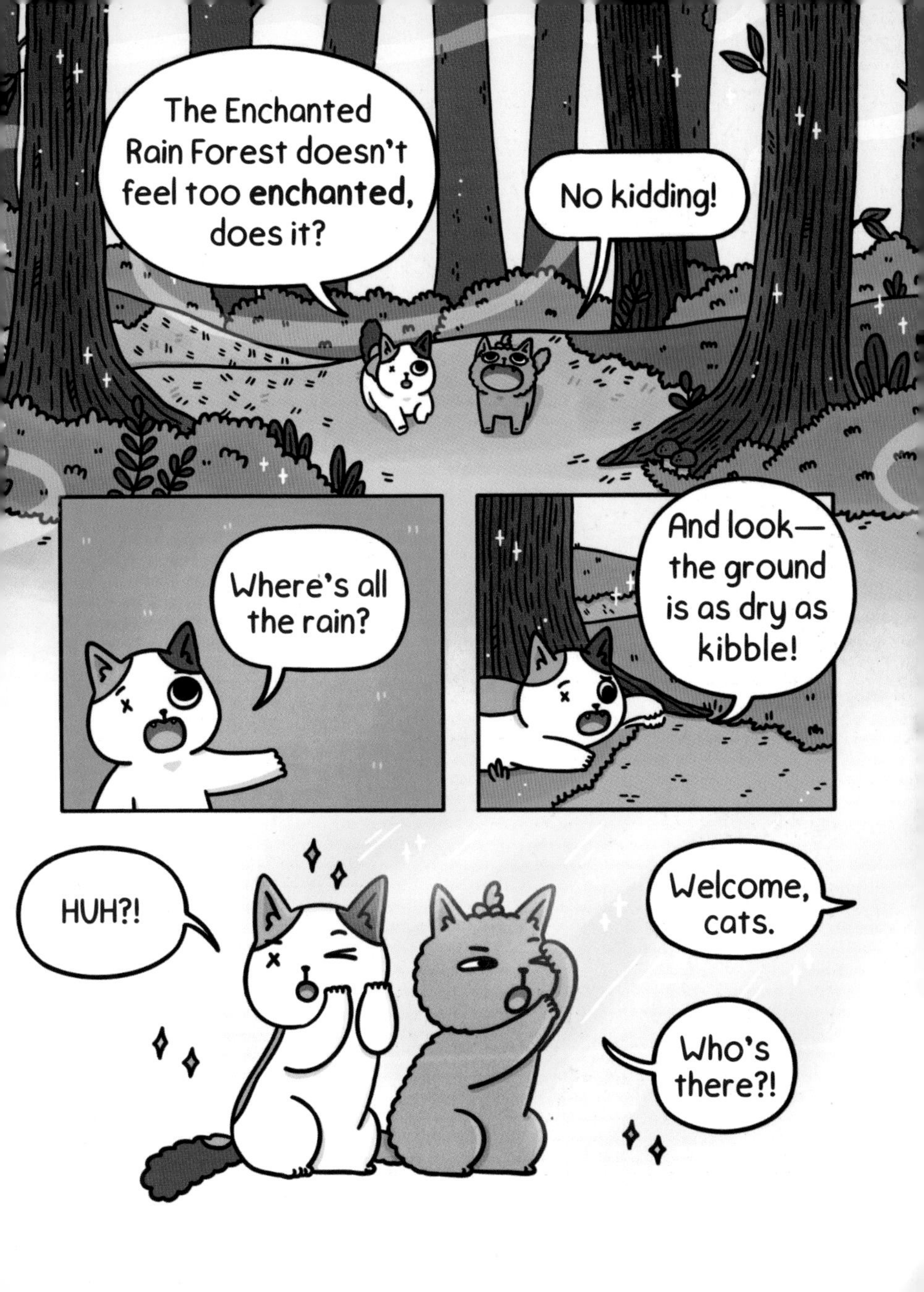
The Enchanted Rain Forest doesn't feel too **enchanted**, does it?
No kidding!
Where's all the rain?
And look—the ground is as dry as kibble!
HUH?!
Welcome, cats.
Who's there?!

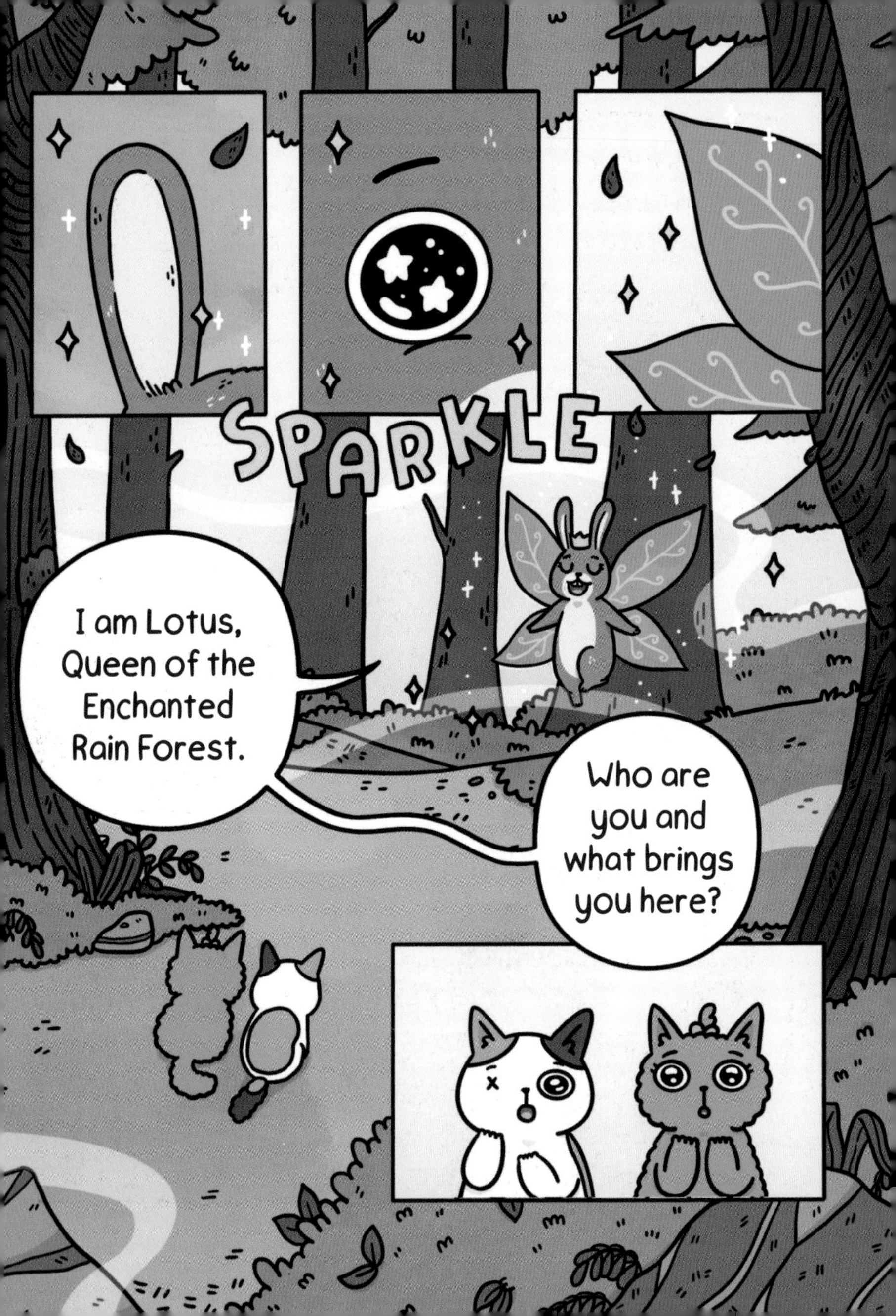
SPARKLE
I am Lotus, Queen of the Enchanted Rain Forest.
Who are you and what brings you here?

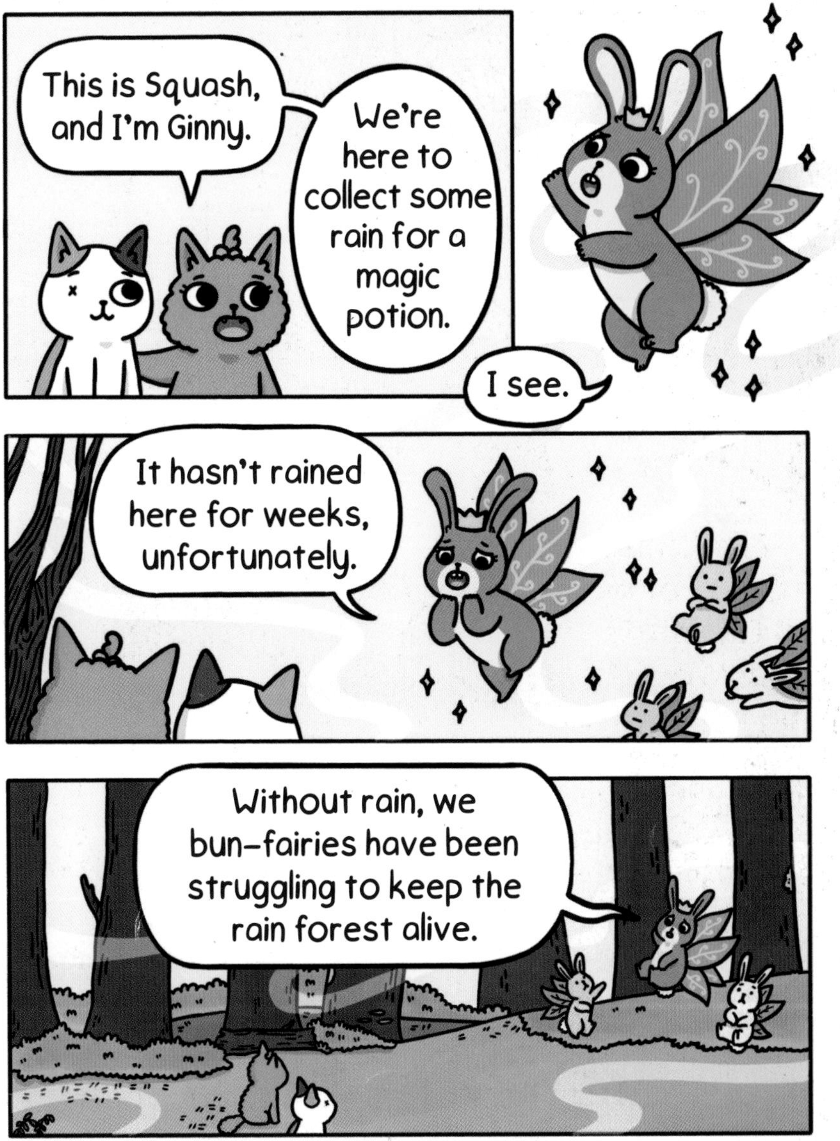
This is Squash, and I'm Ginny.
We're here to collect some rain for a magic potion.
I see.
It hasn't rained here for weeks, unfortunately.
Without rain, we bun-fairies have been struggling to keep the rain forest alive.

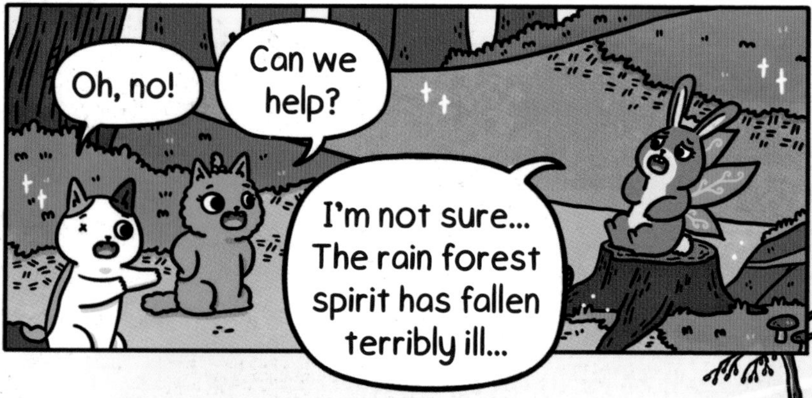
Oh, no!
Can we help?
I'm not sure... The rain forest spirit has fallen terribly ill...

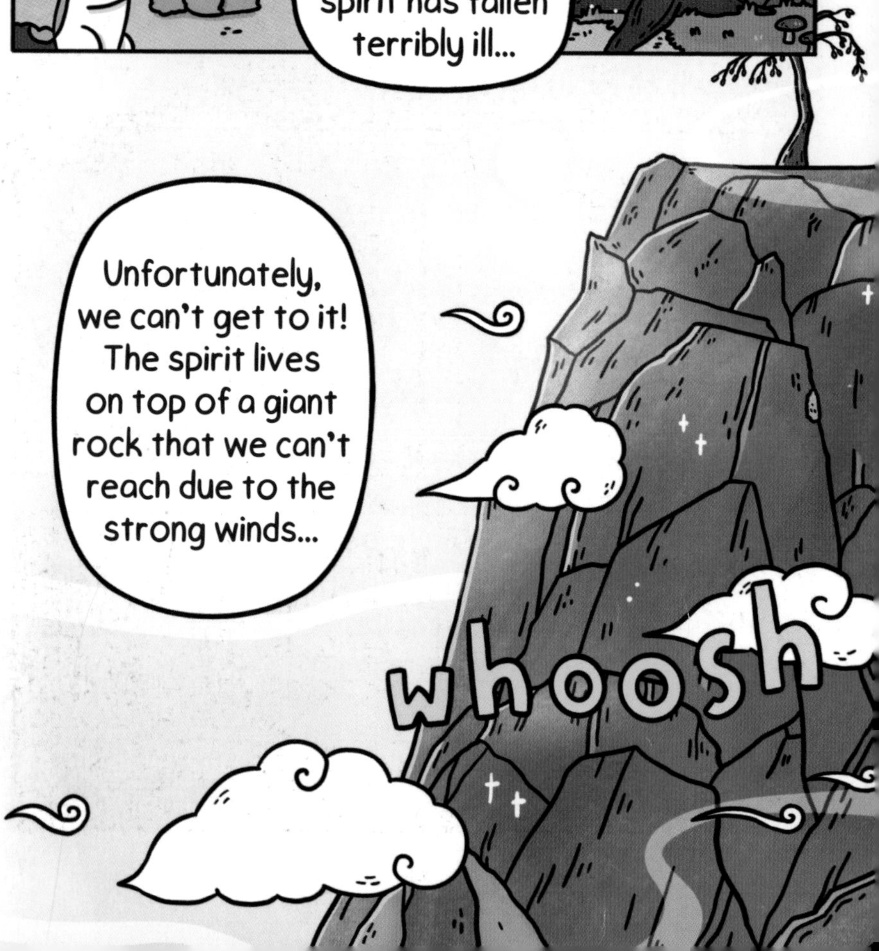
Unfortunately, we can't get to it! The spirit lives on top of a giant rock that we can't reach due to the strong winds...
whoosh

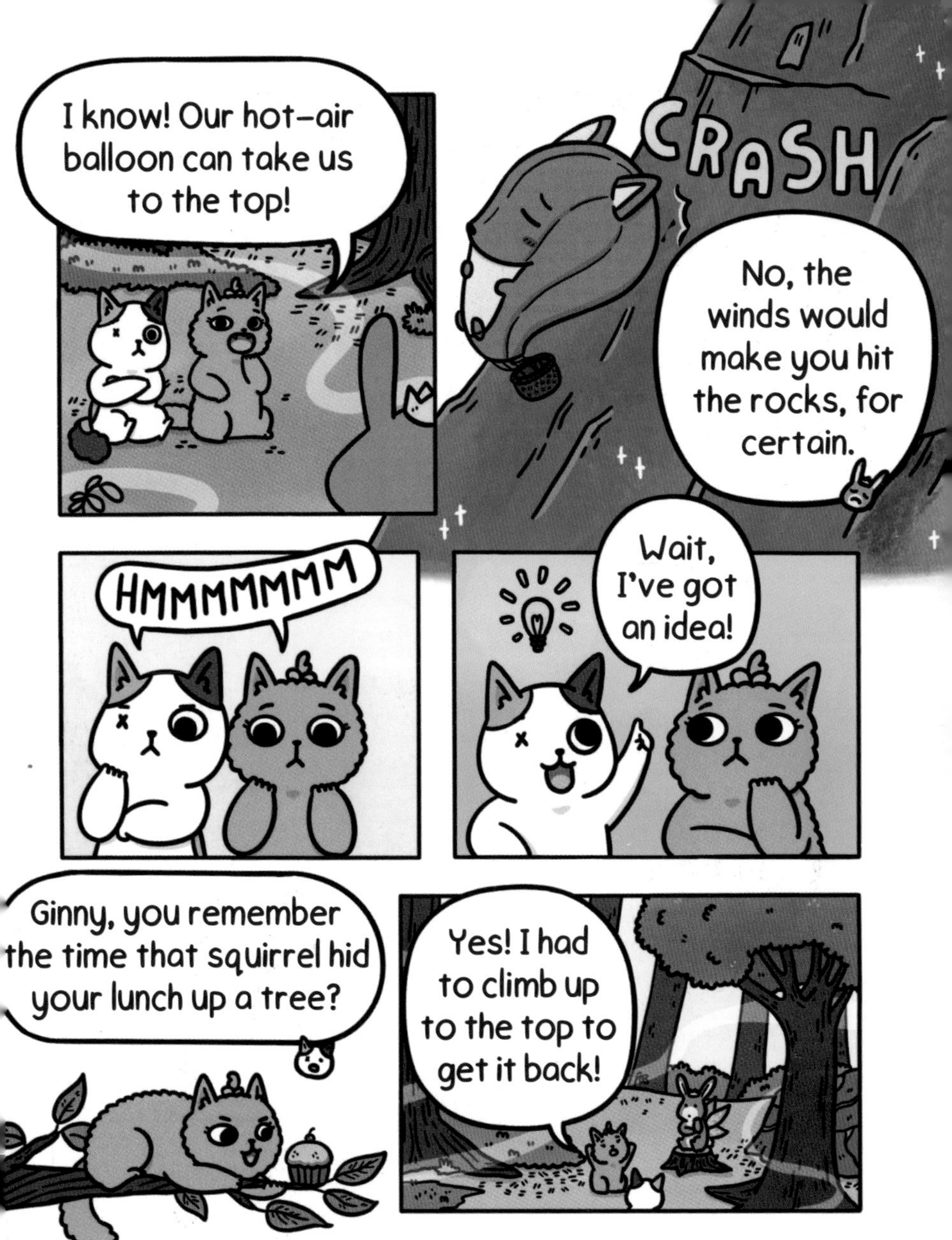
I know! Our hot-air balloon can take us to the top!
CRASH
No, the winds would make you hit the rocks, for certain.
HMMMMMMM
Wait, I've got an idea!
Ginny, you remember the time that squirrel hid your lunch up a tree?
Yes! I had to climb up to the top to get it back!

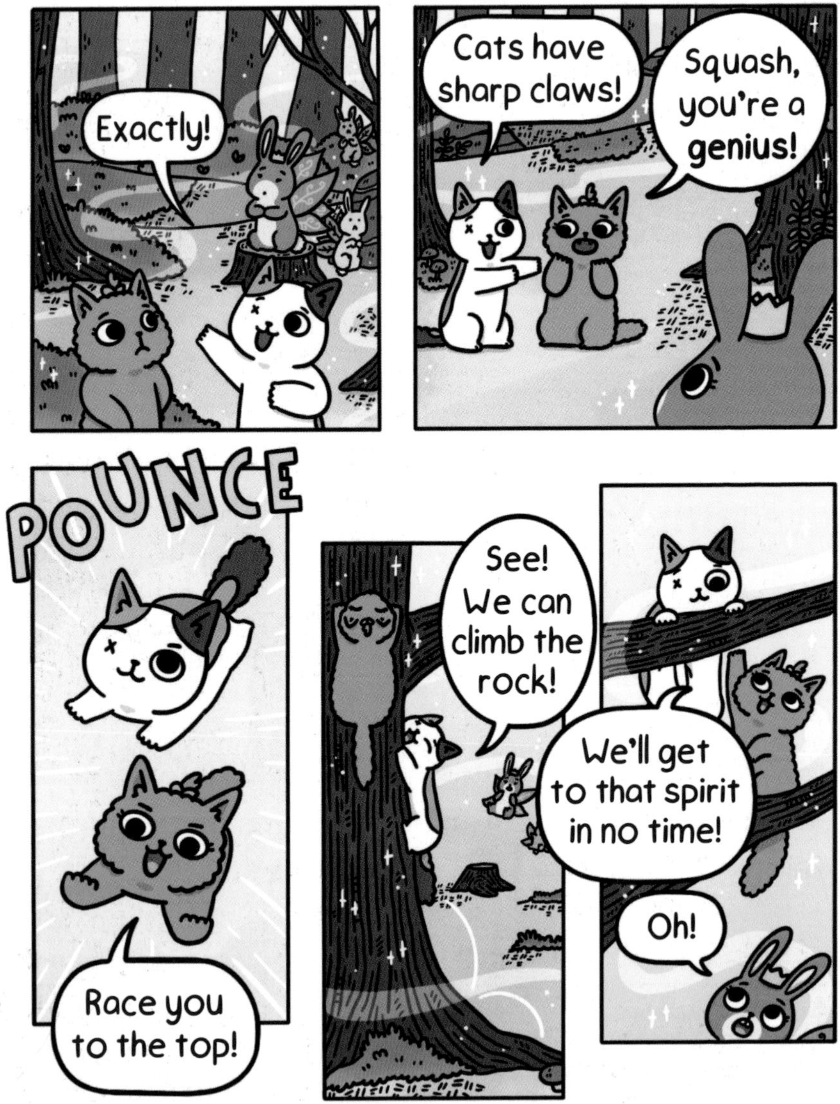

Exactly!
Cats have sharp claws!
Squash, you're a genius!
POUNCE
Race you to the top!
See! We can climb the rock!
We'll get to that spirit in no time!
Oh!

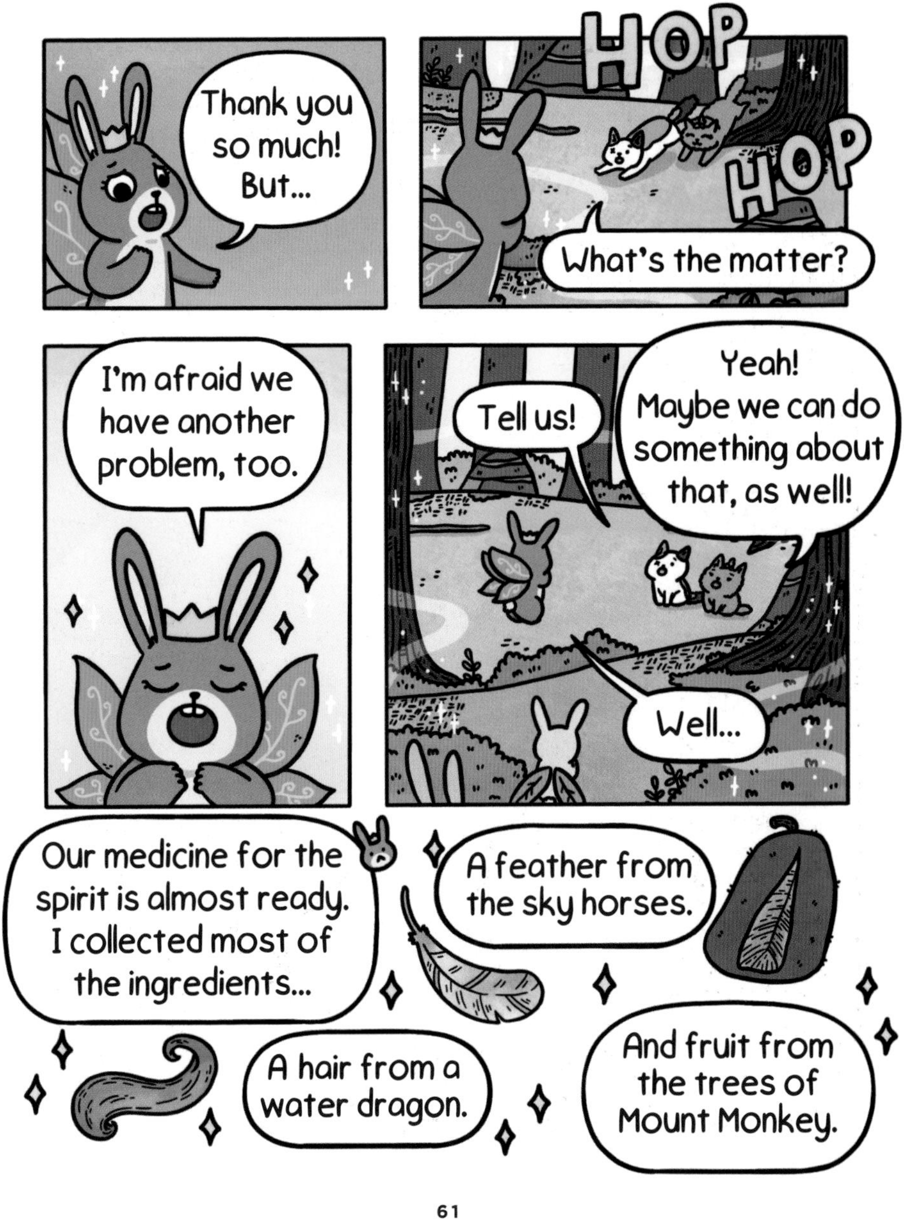
Thank you so much! But...
HOP
HOP
What's the matter?
I'm afraid we have another problem, too.
Tell us!
Yeah! Maybe we can do something about that, as well!
Well...
Our medicine for the spirit is almost ready. I collected most of the ingredients...
A feather from the sky horses.
A hair from a water dragon.
And fruit from the trees of Mount Monkey.

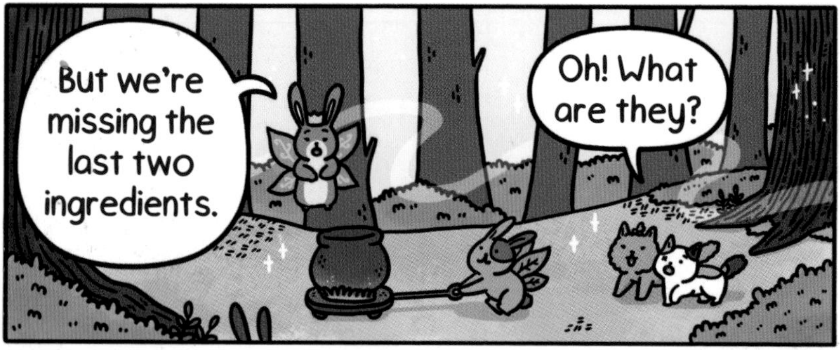
But we're missing the last two ingredients.
Oh! What are they?

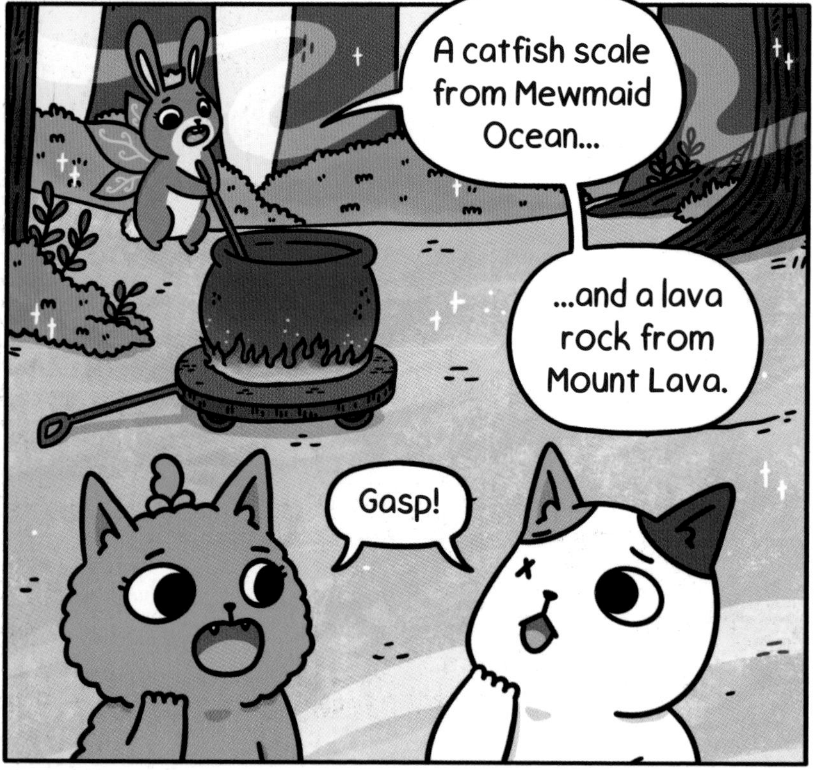
A catfish scale from Mewmaid Ocean...
...and a lava rock from Mount Lava.
Gasp!

CHAPTER FIVE: Spirit

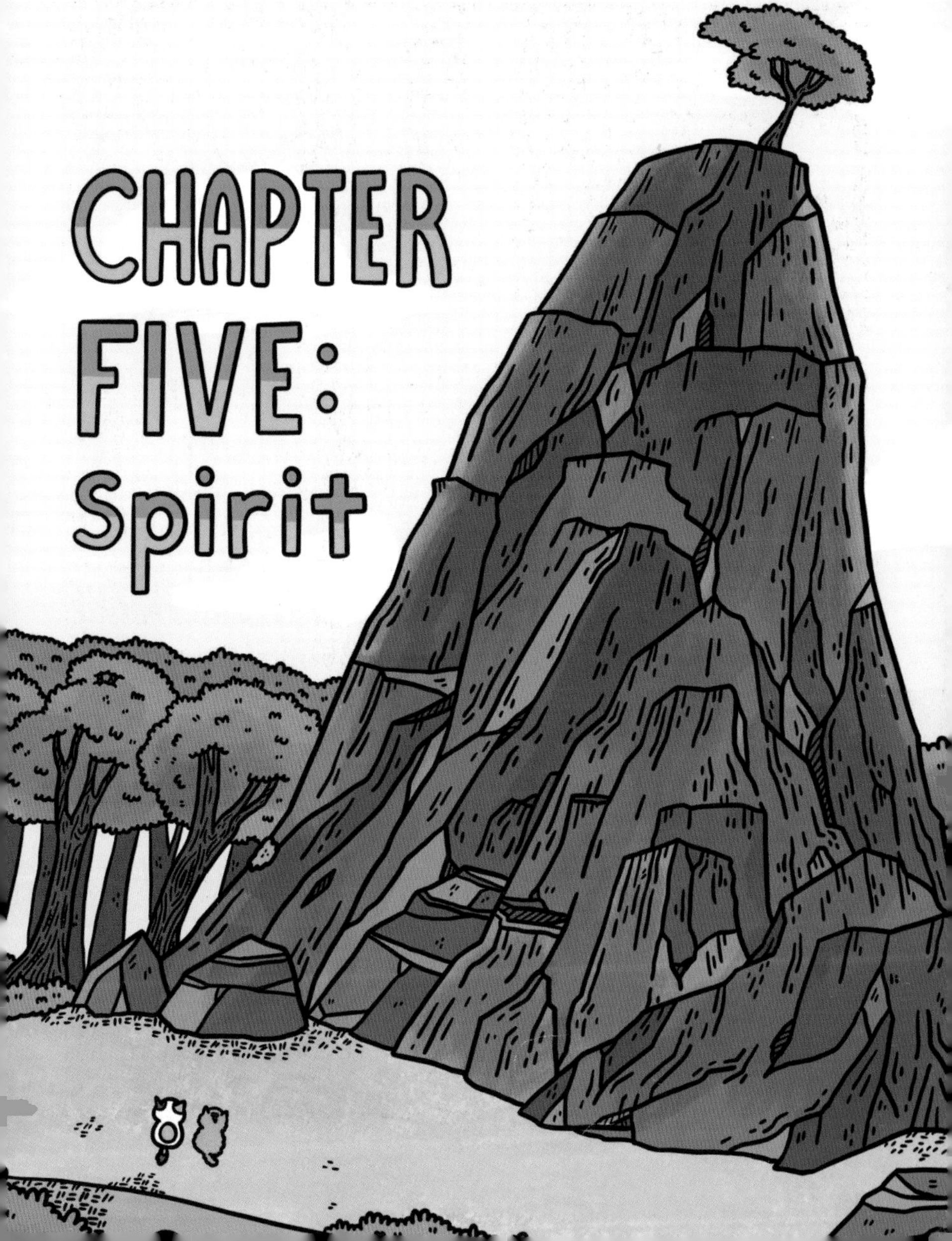

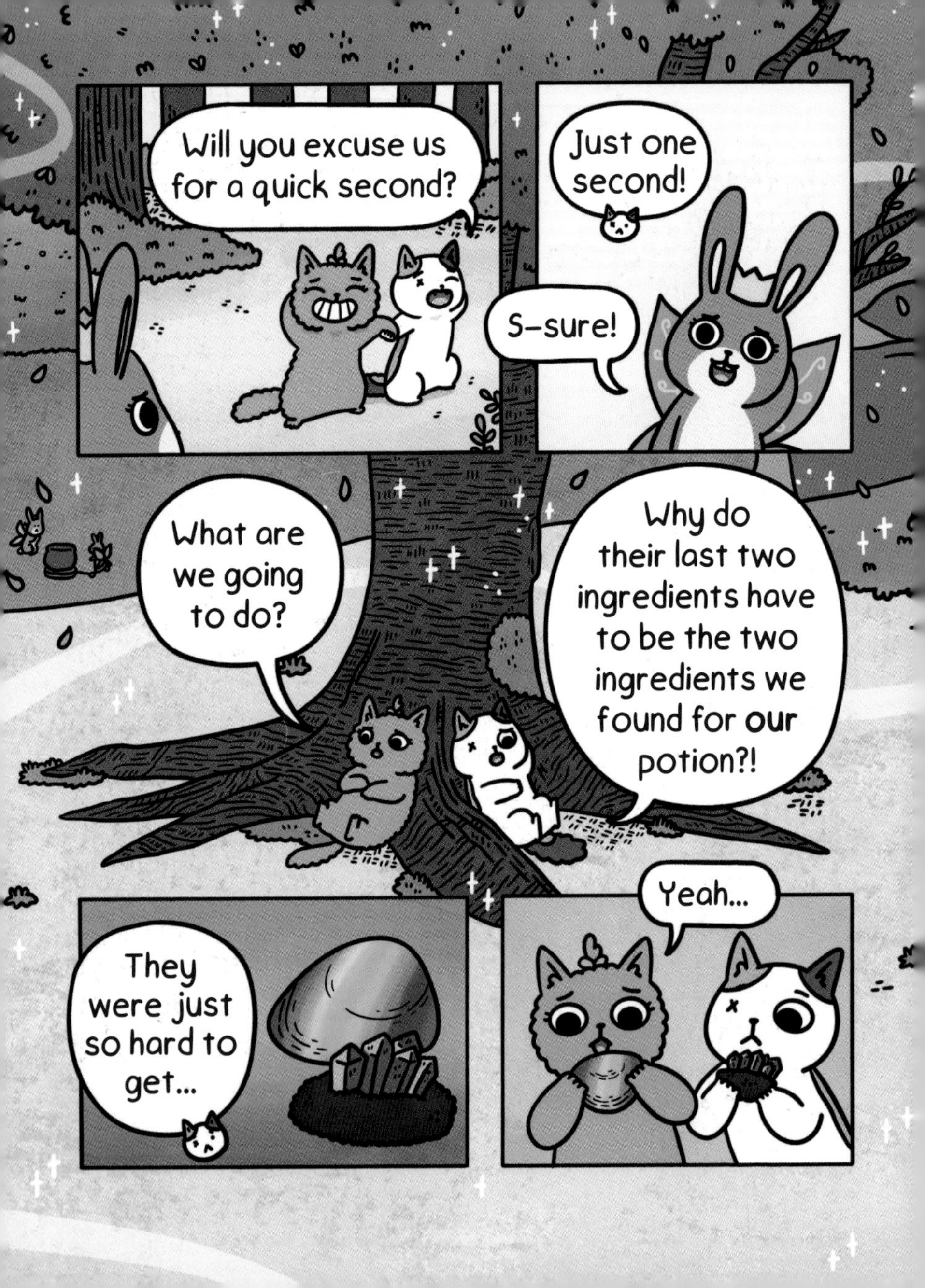
Will you excuse us for a quick second?
Just one second!
S-sure!
What are we going to do?
Why do their last two ingredients have to be the two ingredients we found for **our** potion?!
They were just so hard to get...
Yeah...

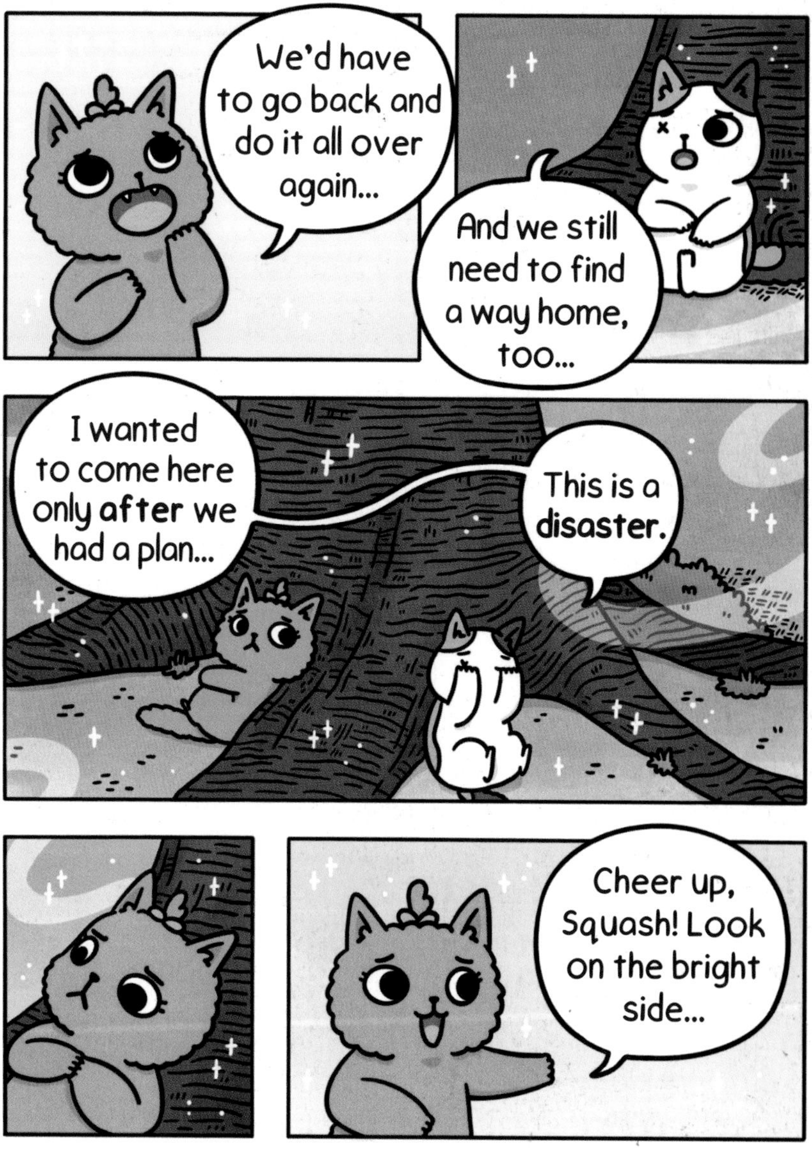
We'd have to go back and do it all over again...
And we still need to find a way home, too...
I wanted to come here only **after** we had a plan...
This is a **disaster.**
Cheer up, Squash! Look on the bright side...

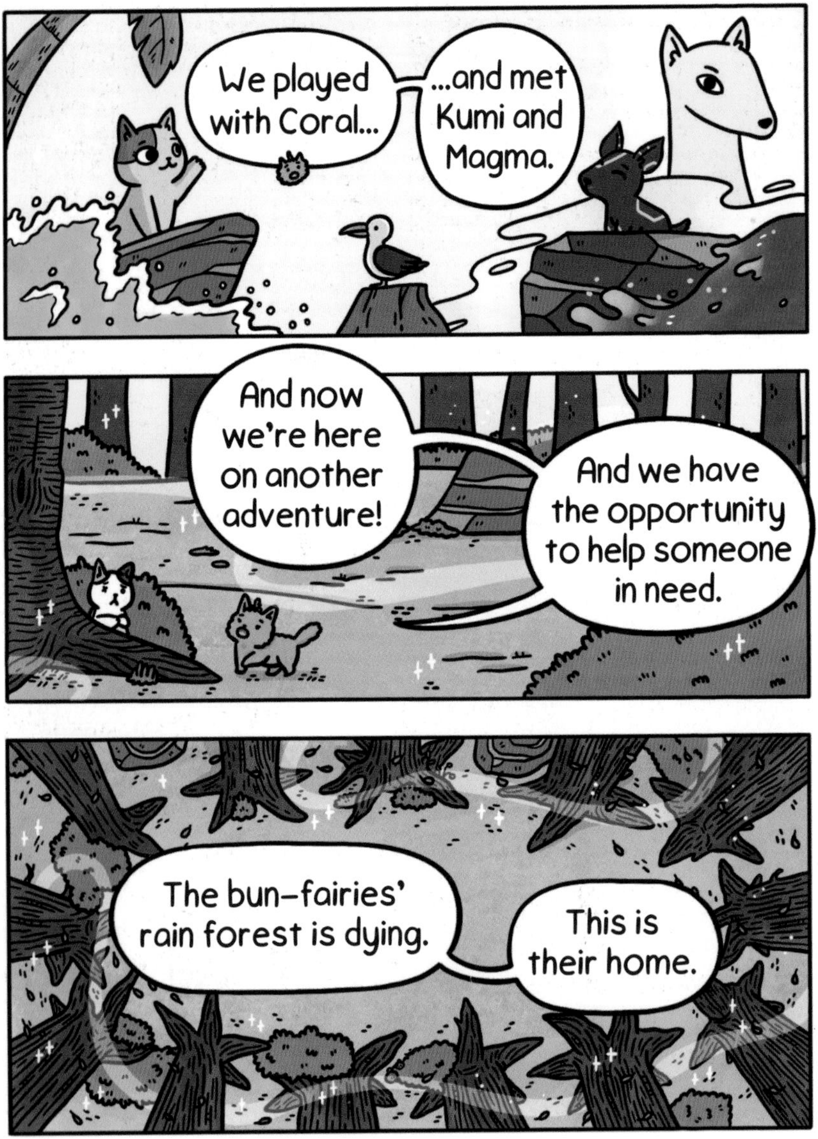
We played with Coral...
...and met Kumi and Magma.
And now we're here on another adventure!
And we have the opportunity to help someone in need.
The bun-fairies' rain forest is dying.
This is their home.

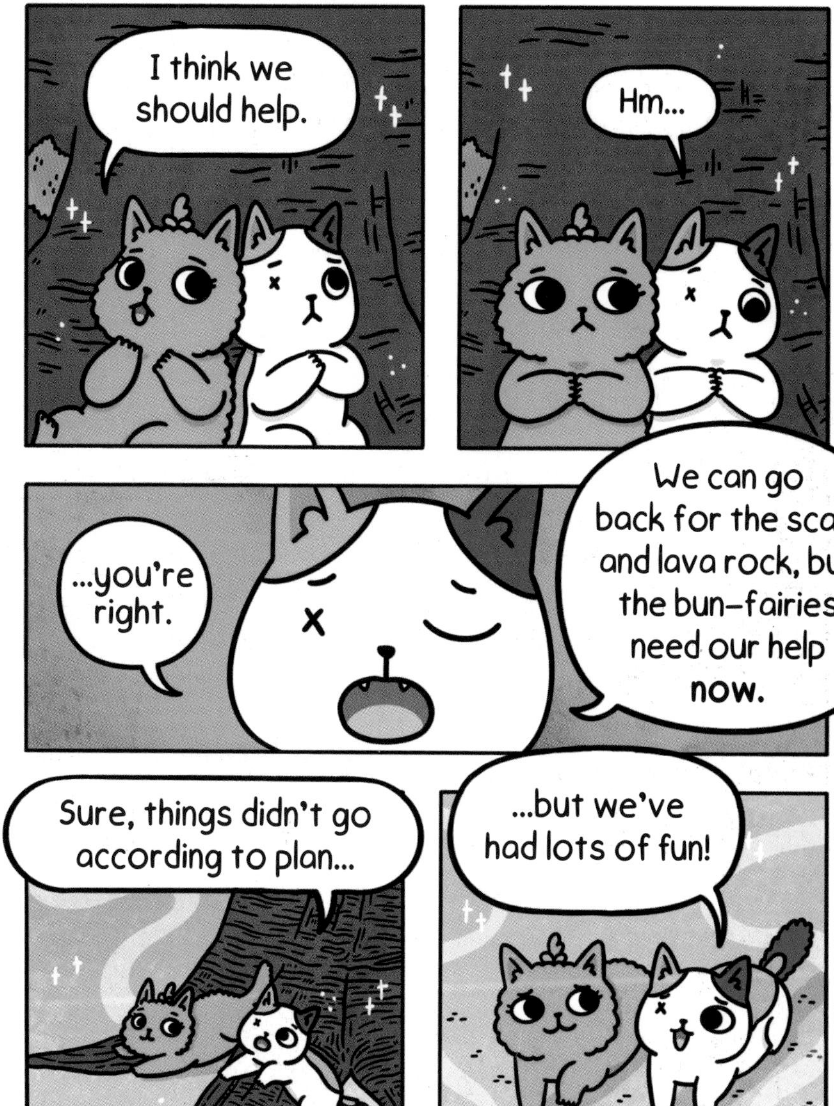
I think we should help.
Hm...
...you're right.
We can go back for the scale and lava rock, but the bun-fairies need our help **now.**
Sure, things didn't go according to plan...
...but we've had lots of fun!

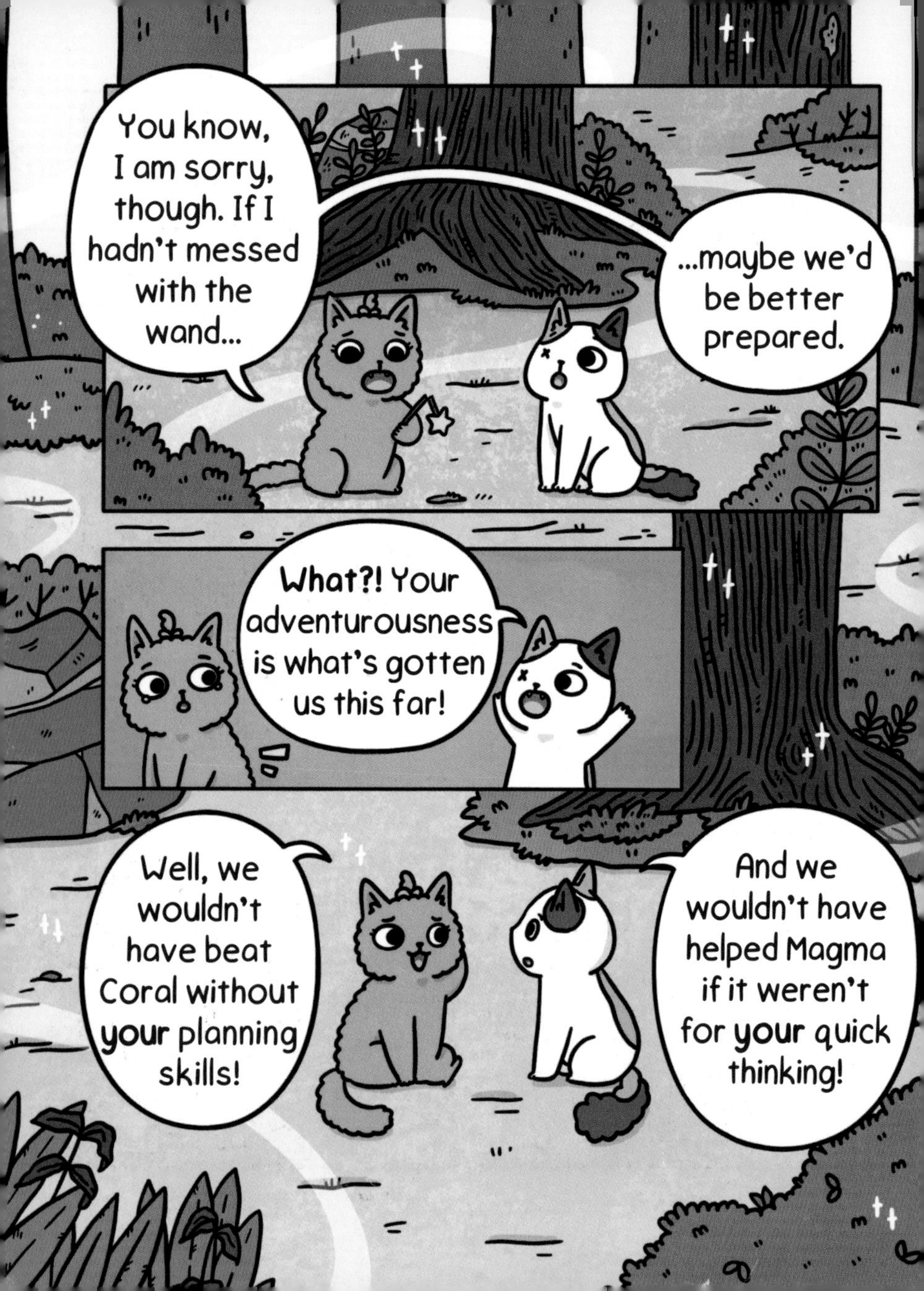
You know, I am sorry, though. If I hadn't messed with the wand...
...maybe we'd be better prepared.
What?! Your adventurousness is what's gotten us this far!
Well, we wouldn't have beat Coral without **your** planning skills!
And we wouldn't have helped Magma if it weren't for **your** quick thinking!

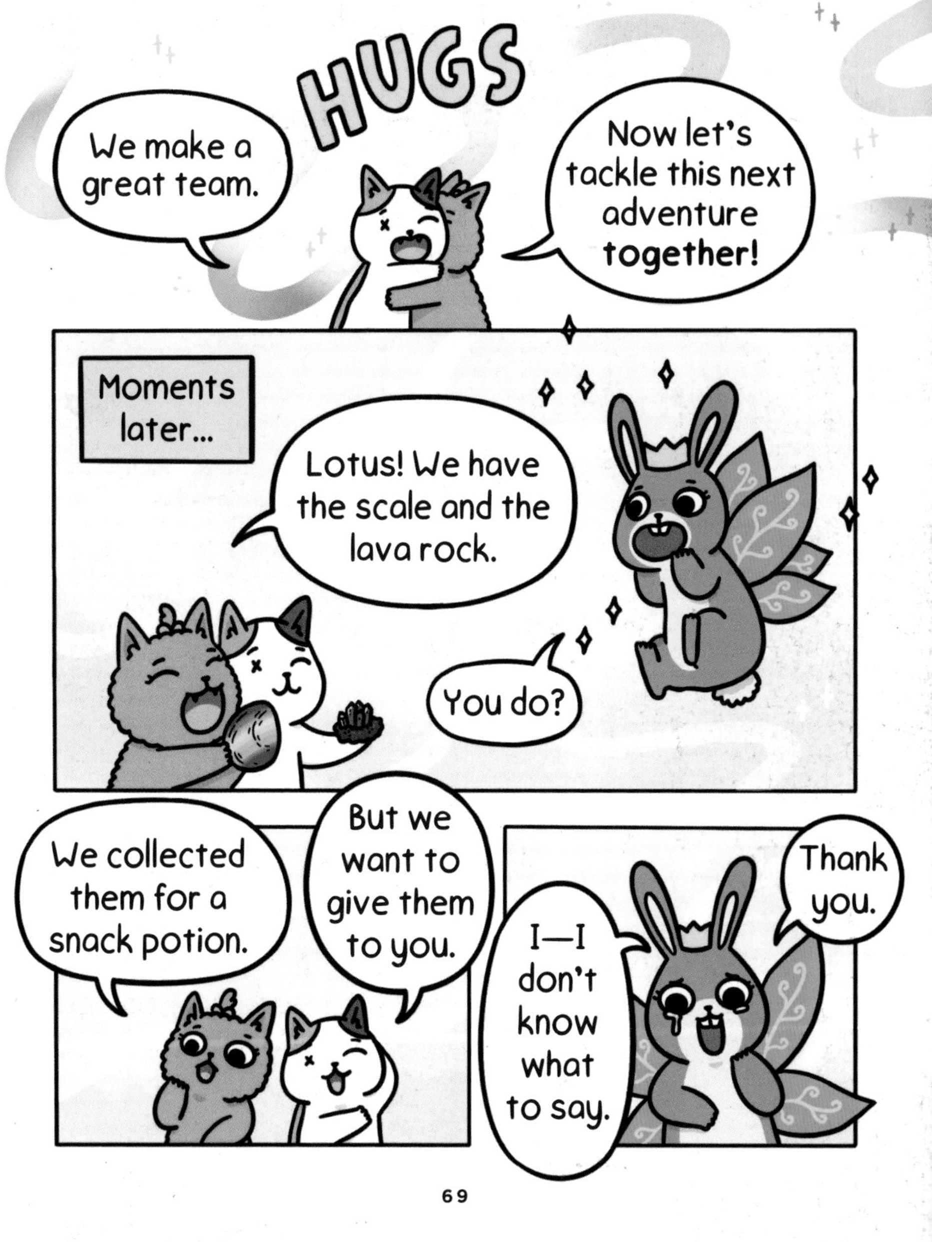
HUGS
We make a great team.
Now let's tackle this next adventure together!
Moments later...
Lotus! We have the scale and the lava rock.
You do?
We collected them for a snack potion.
But we want to give them to you.
I—I don't know what to say.
Thank you.

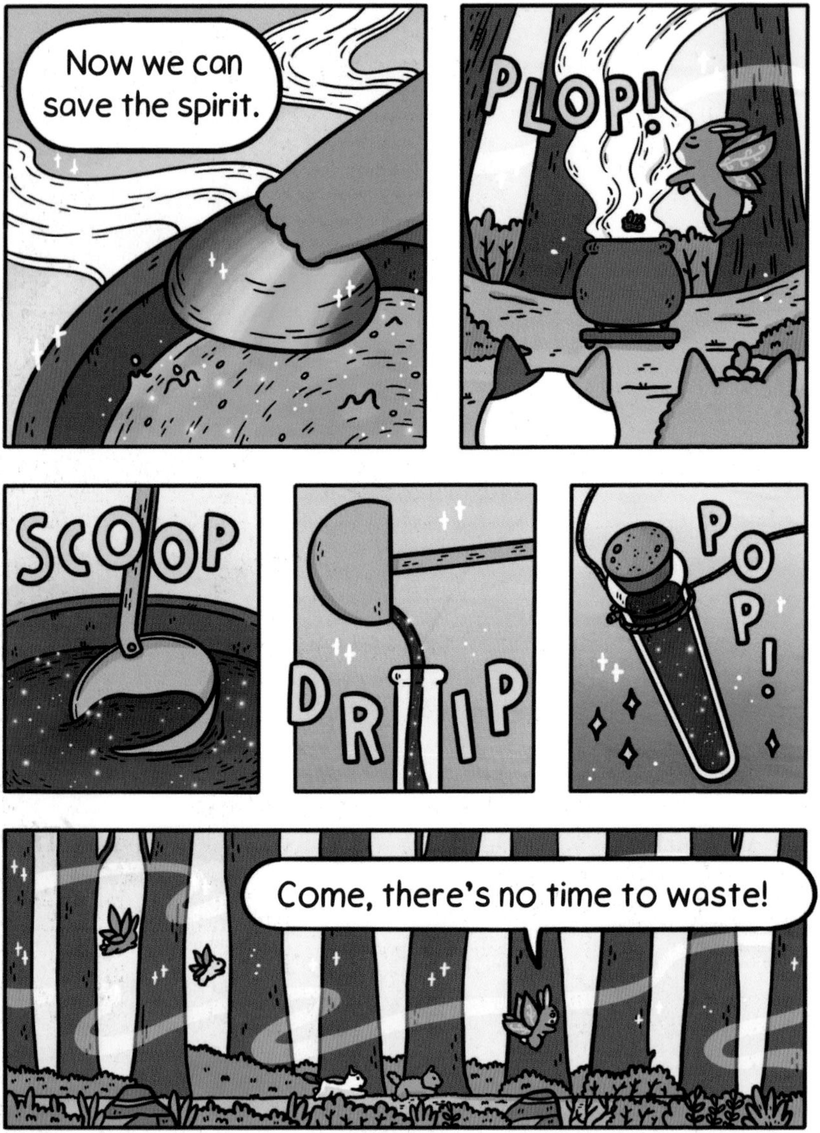
Now we can save the spirit.
PLOP!
SCOOP
DRIP
POP!
Come, there's no time to waste!

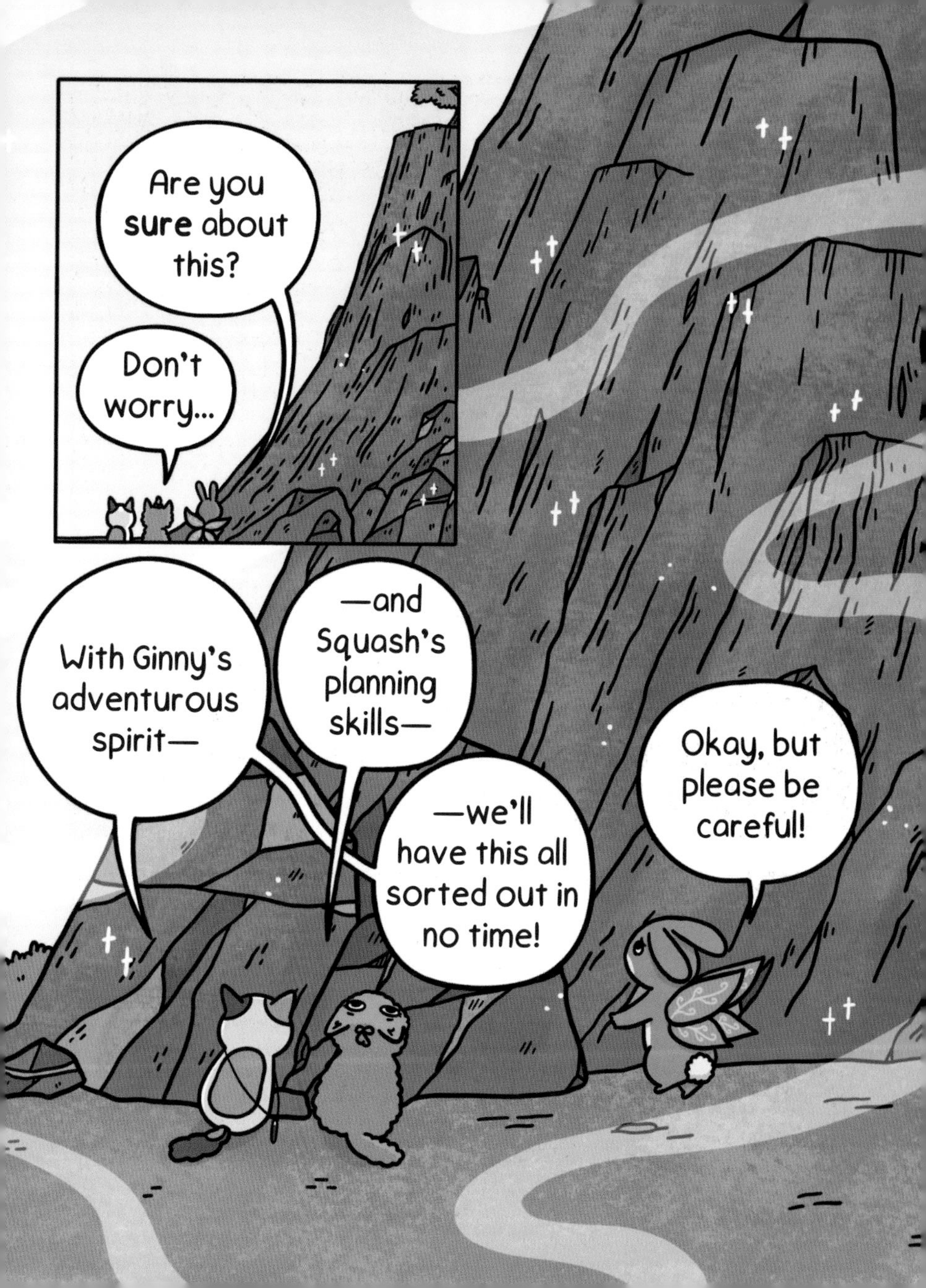
Are you **sure** about this?
Don't worry...
With Ginny's adventurous spirit—
—and Squash's planning skills—
—we'll have this all sorted out in no time!
Okay, but please be careful!

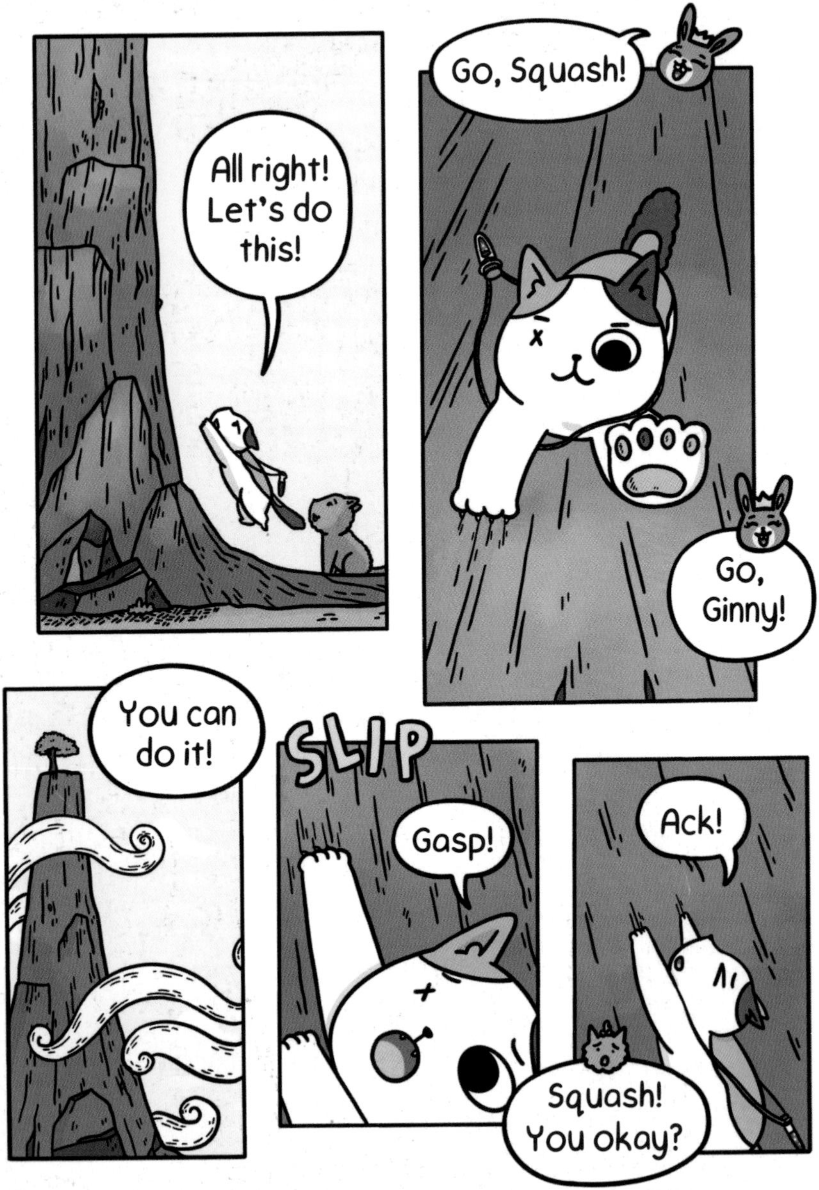
All right! Let's do this!
Go, Squash!
Go, Ginny!
You can do it!
SLIP
Gasp!
Ack!
Squash! You okay?

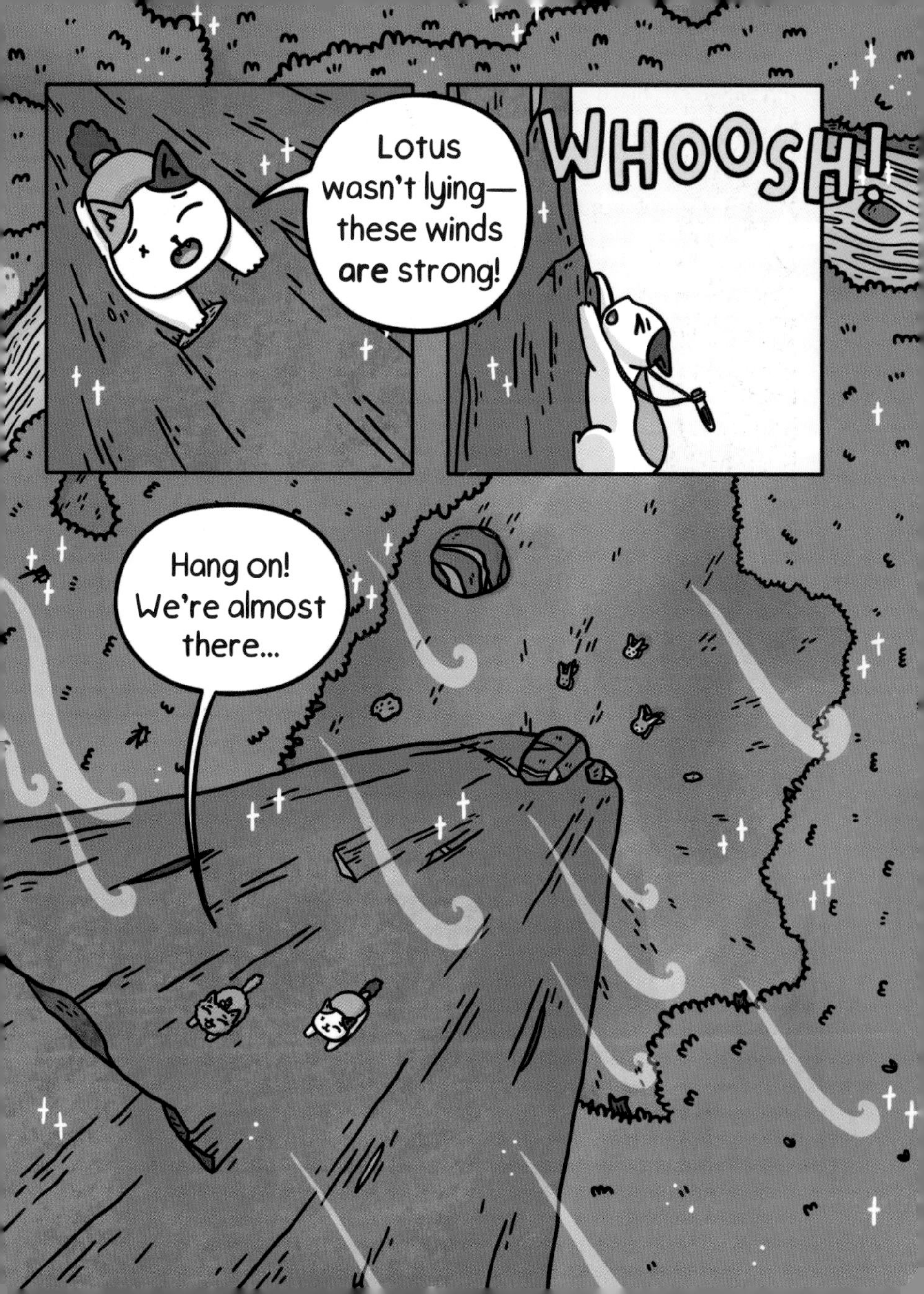
Lotus wasn't lying—these winds are strong!
WHOOSH!
Hang on! We're almost there...

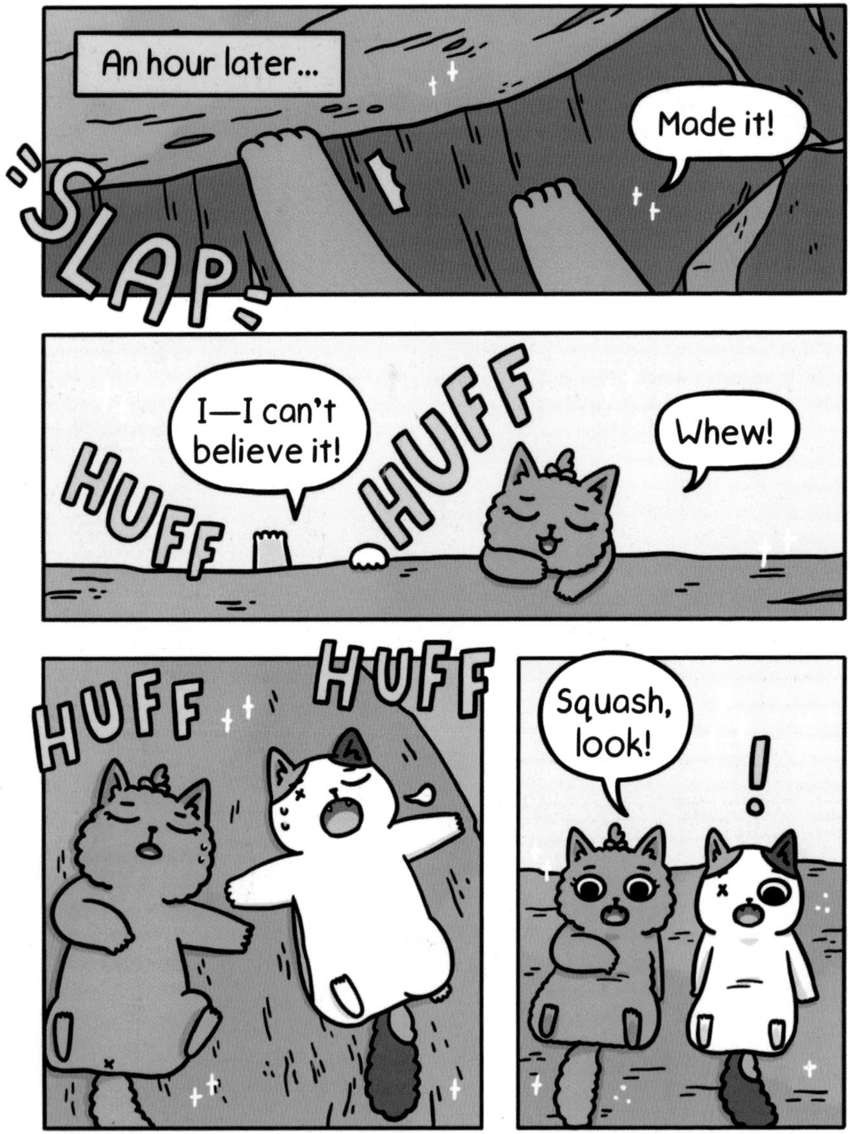
An hour later...
SLAP
Made it!
HUFF
I—I can't believe it!
HUFF
Whew!
HUFF
HUFF
Squash, look!
!

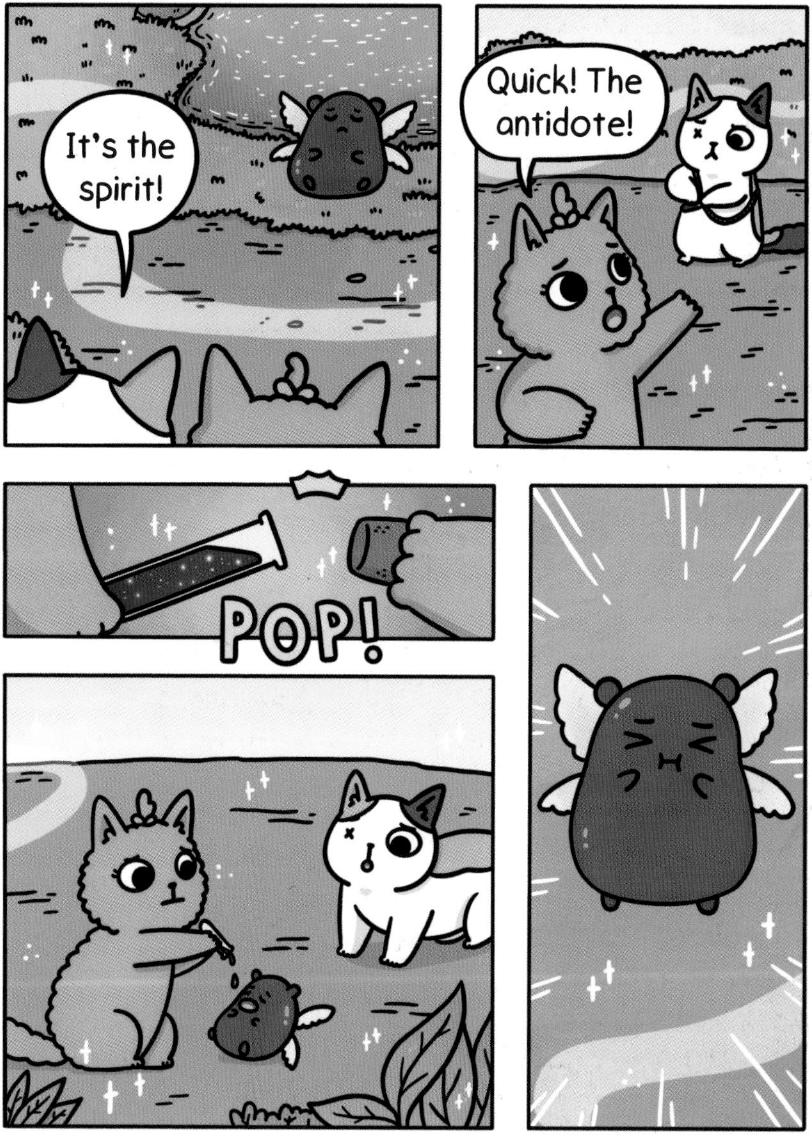
It's the spirit!
Quick! The antidote!
POP!

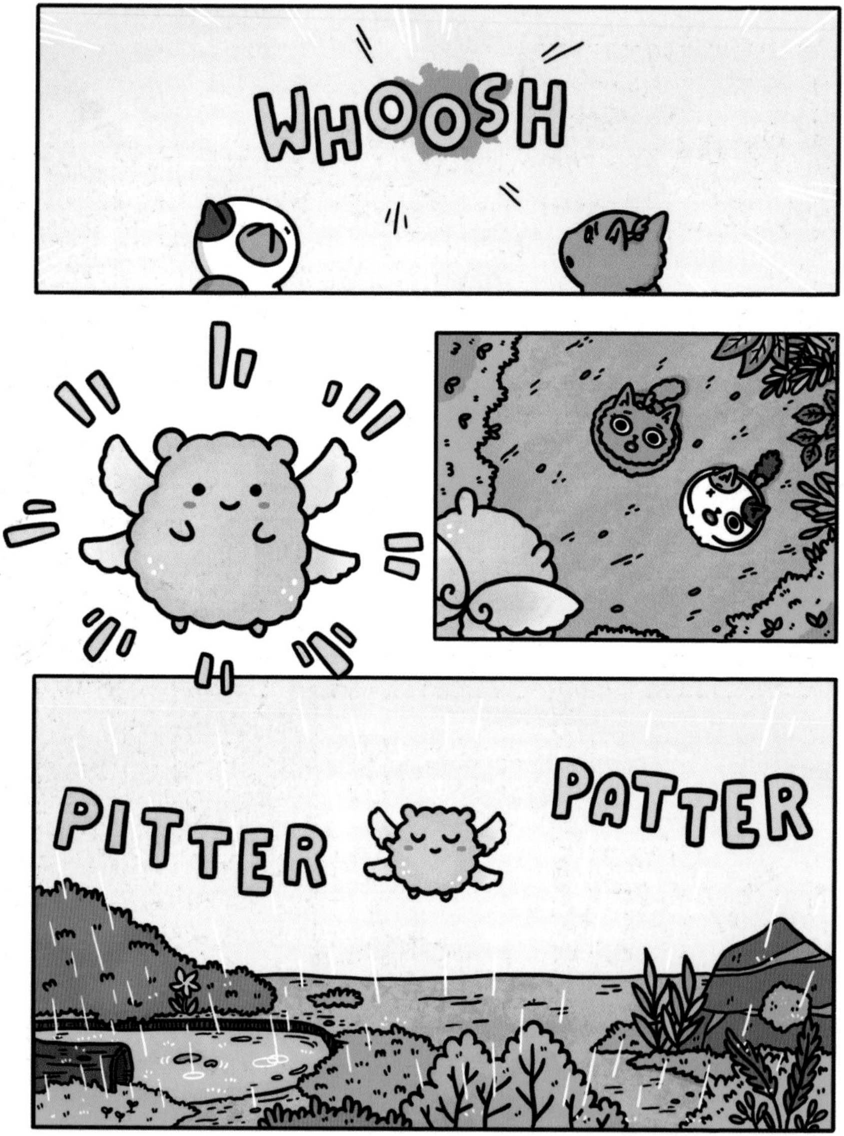
WHOOSH
PITTER
PATTER

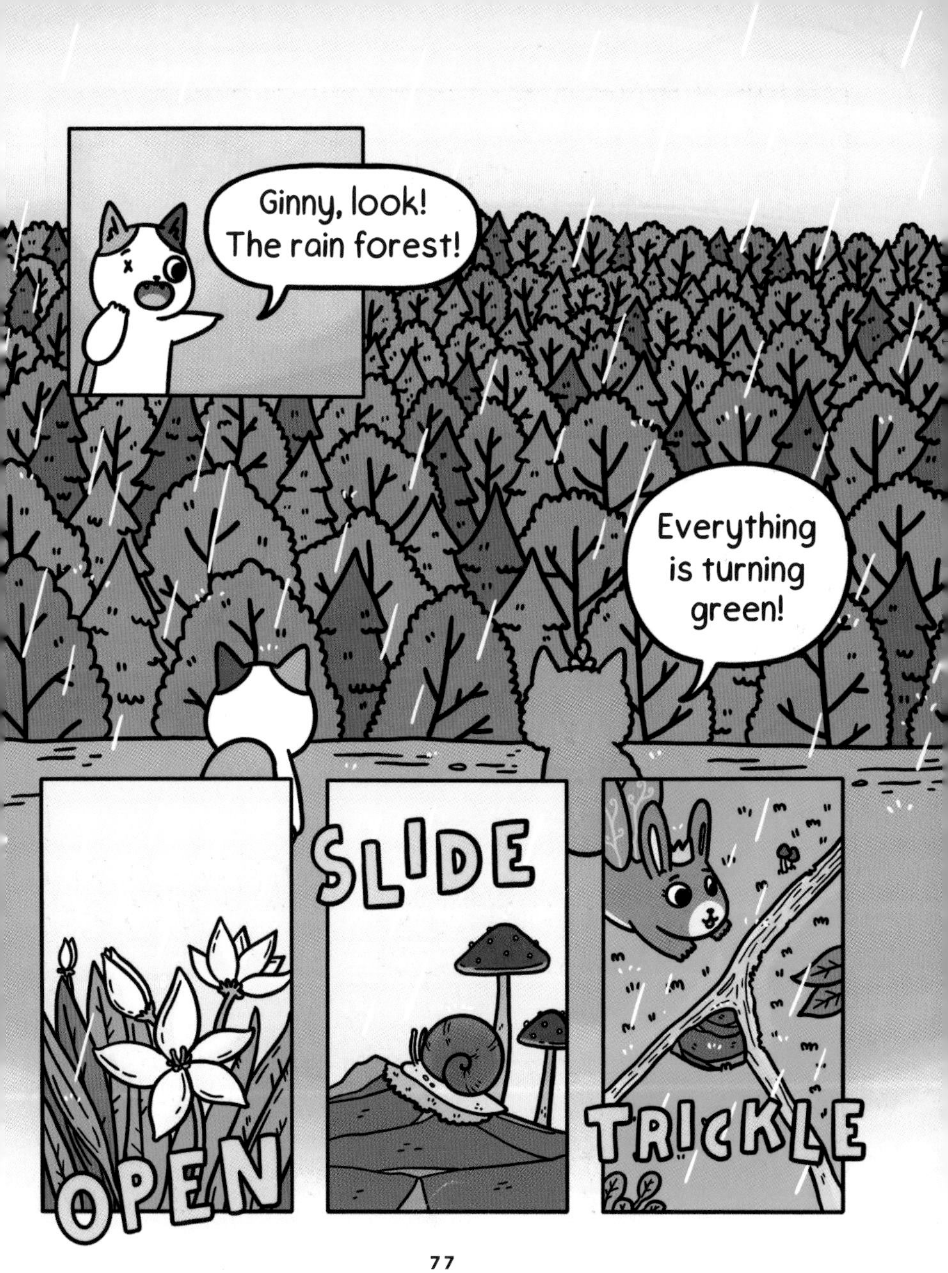
Ginny, look! The rain forest!
Everything is turning green!
SLIDE
TRICKLE
OPEN

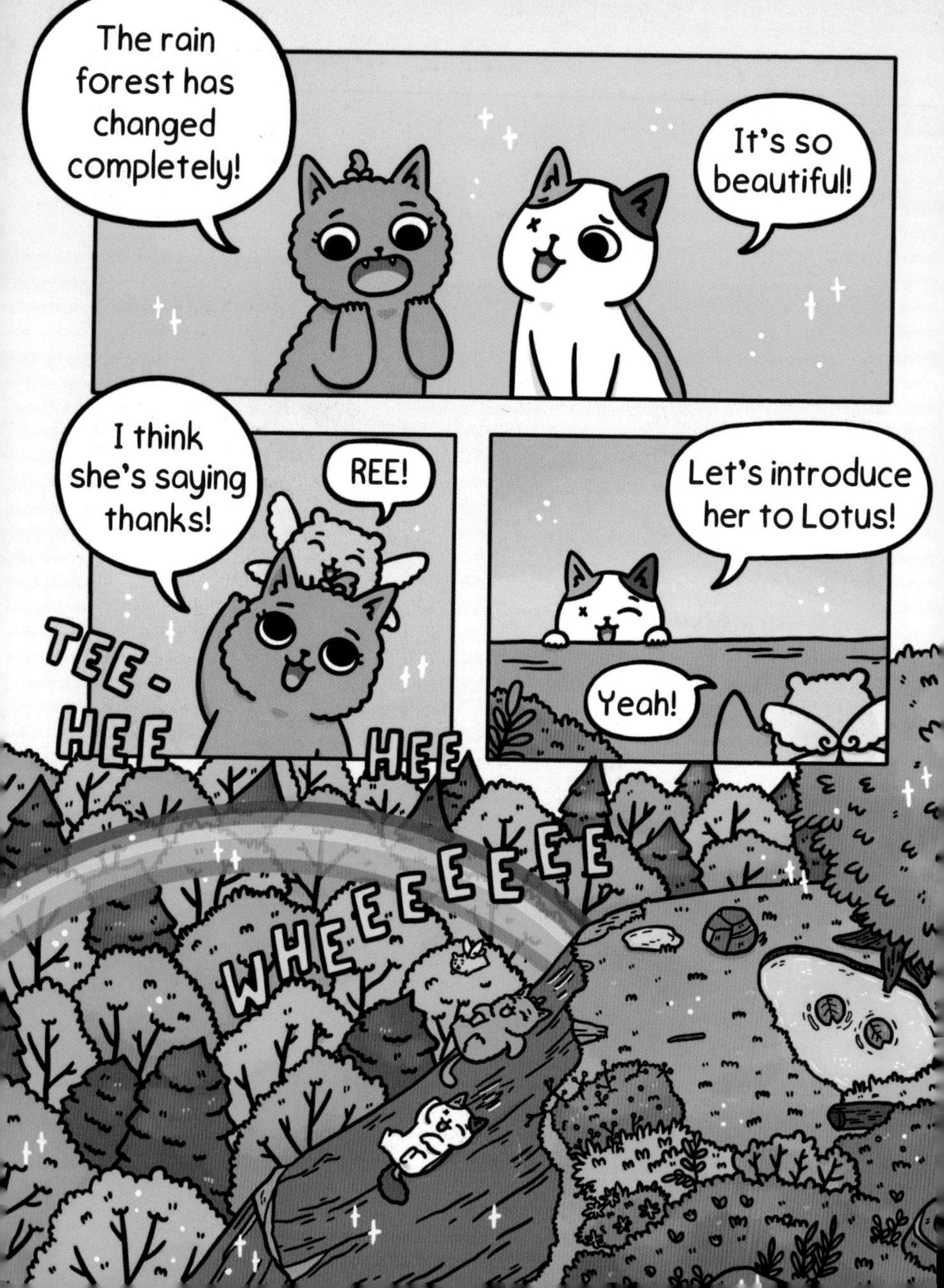
The rain forest has changed completely!
It's so beautiful!
I think she's saying thanks!
REE!
TEE-HEE
HEE
Let's introduce her to Lotus!
Yeah!
WHEEEEEEEE

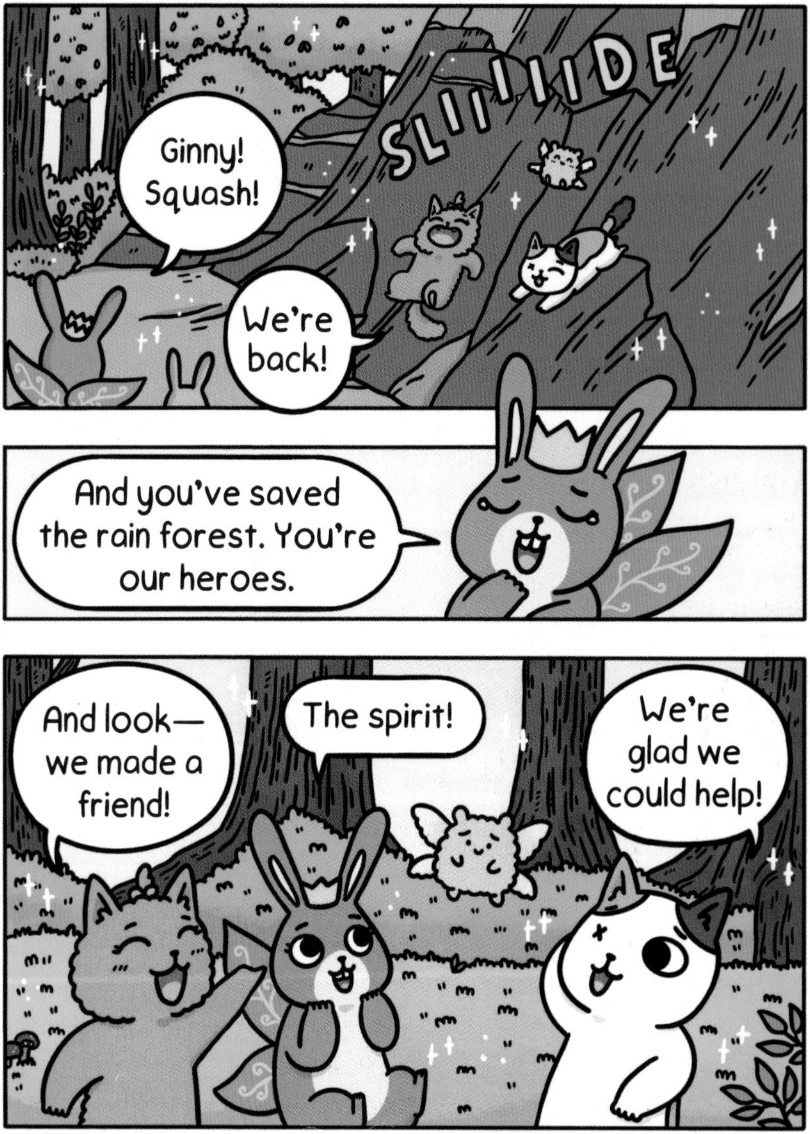
SLIIIIIDE
Ginny! Squash!
We're back!
And you've saved the rain forest. You're our heroes.
And look—we made a friend!
The spirit!
We're glad we could help!

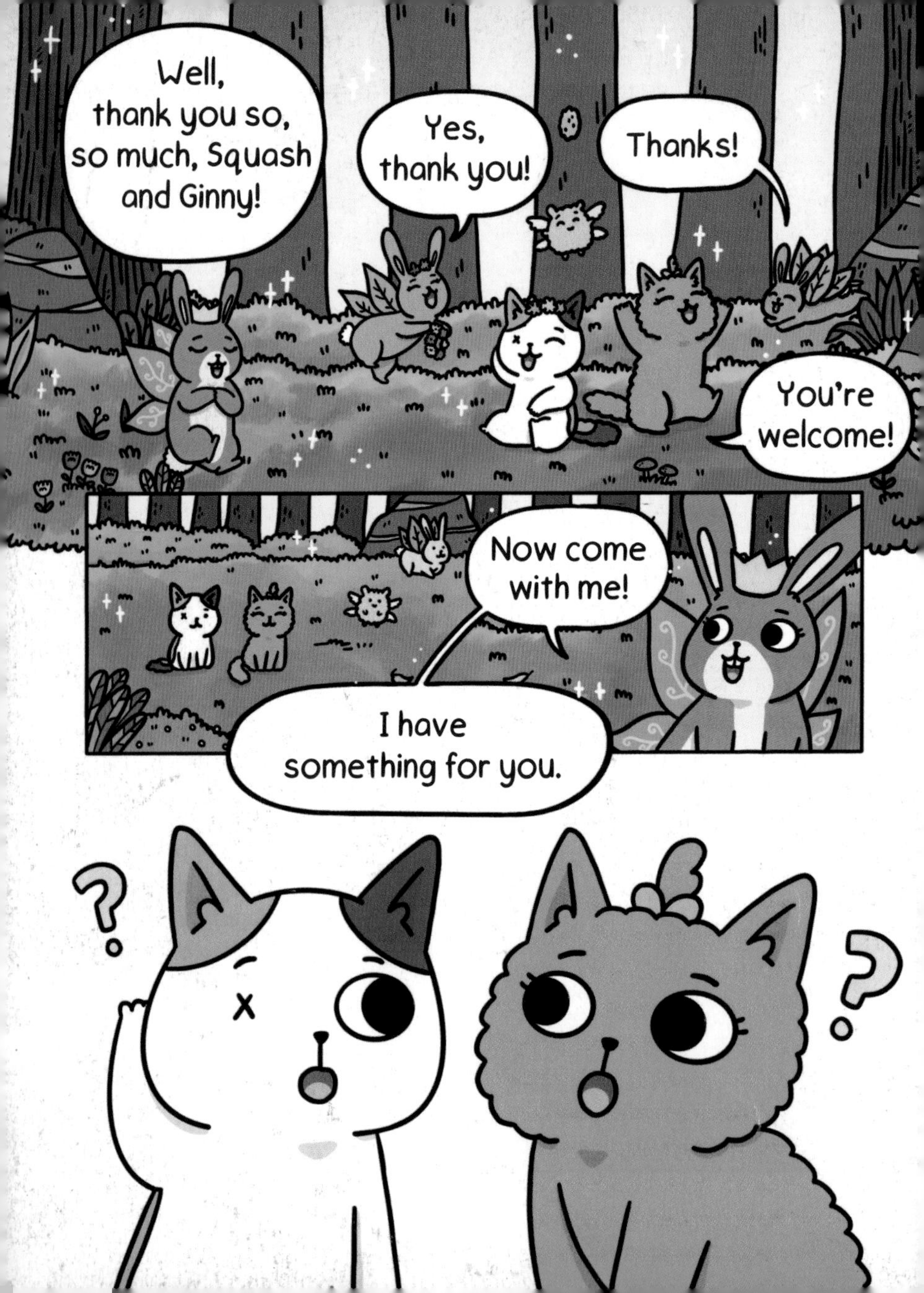
Well, thank you so, so much, Squash and Ginny!
Yes, thank you!
Thanks!
You're welcome!
Now come with me!
I have something for you.
?
?

CHAPTER SIX: Home

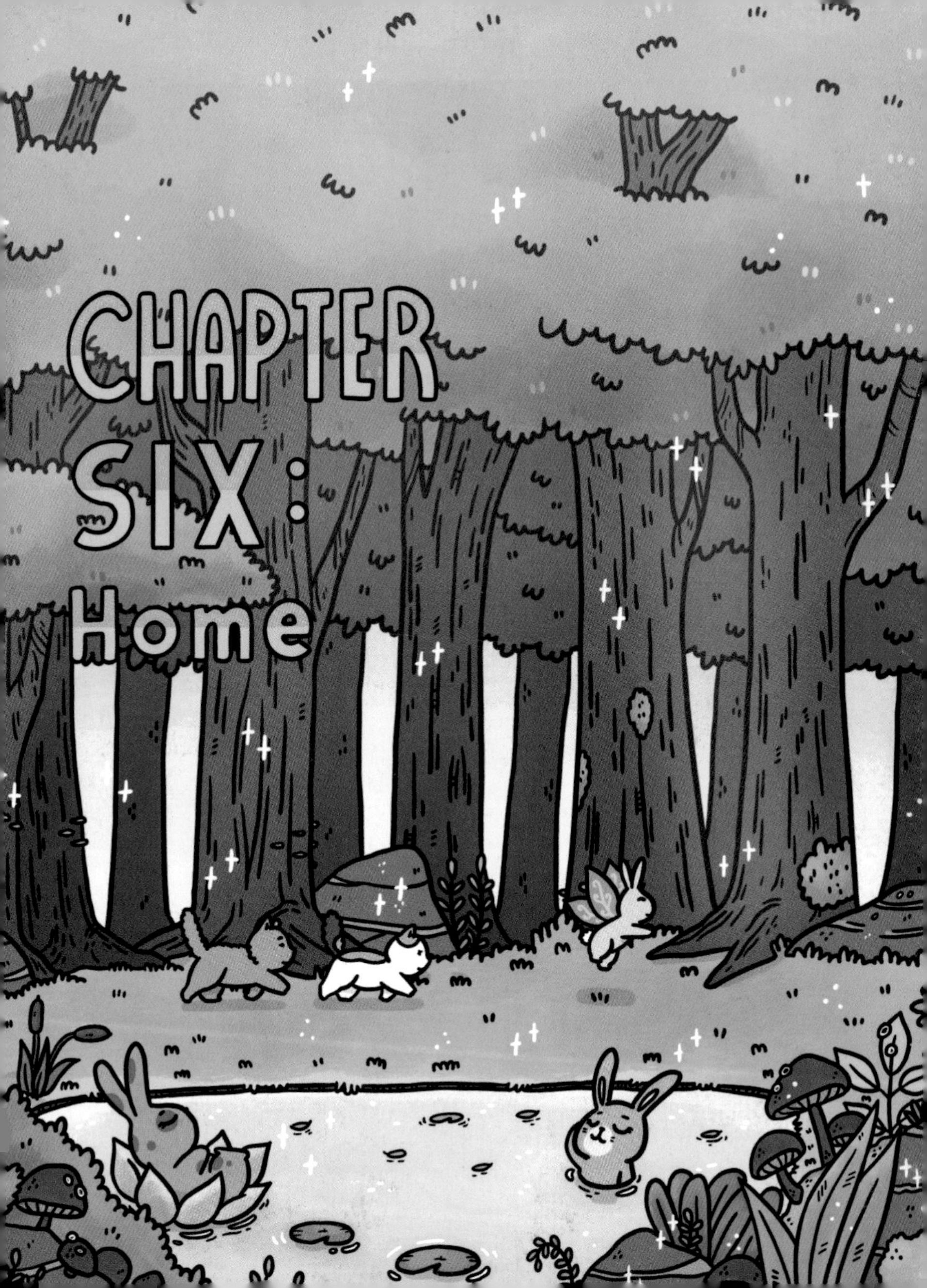

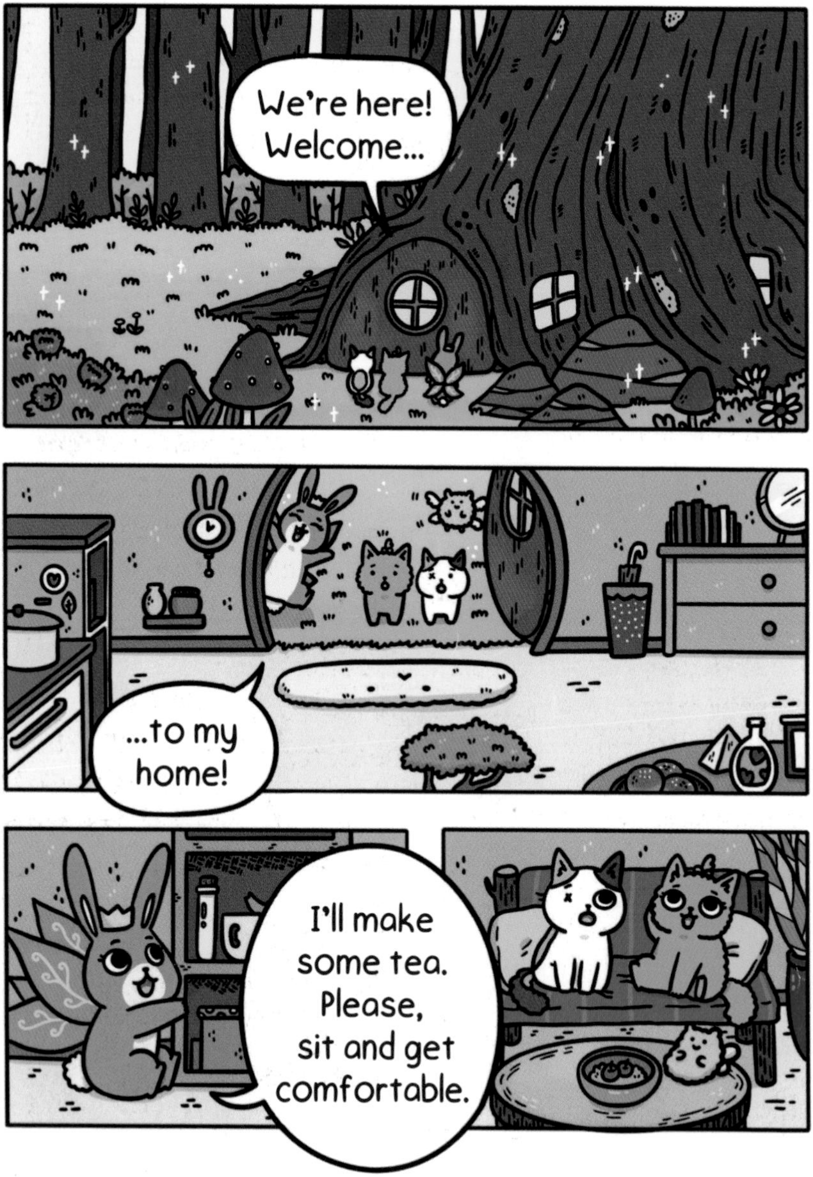
We're here! Welcome...
...to my home!
I'll make some tea. Please, sit and get comfortable.

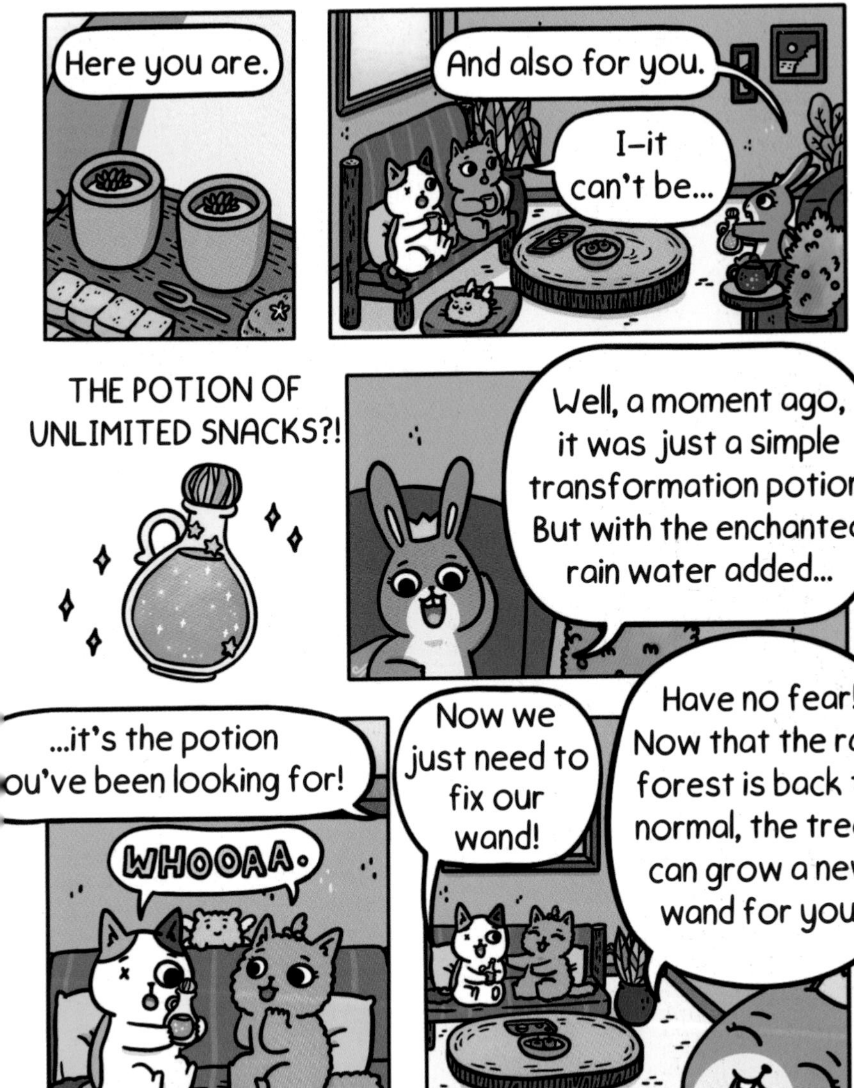

Here you are.
And also for you.
I–it can't be...
THE POTION OF UNLIMITED SNACKS?!
Well, a moment ago, it was just a simple transformation potion. But with the enchanted rain water added...
...it's the potion ou've been looking for!
WHOOAA.
Now we just need to fix our wand!
Have no fear! Now that the rain forest is back to normal, the trees can grow a new wand for you.

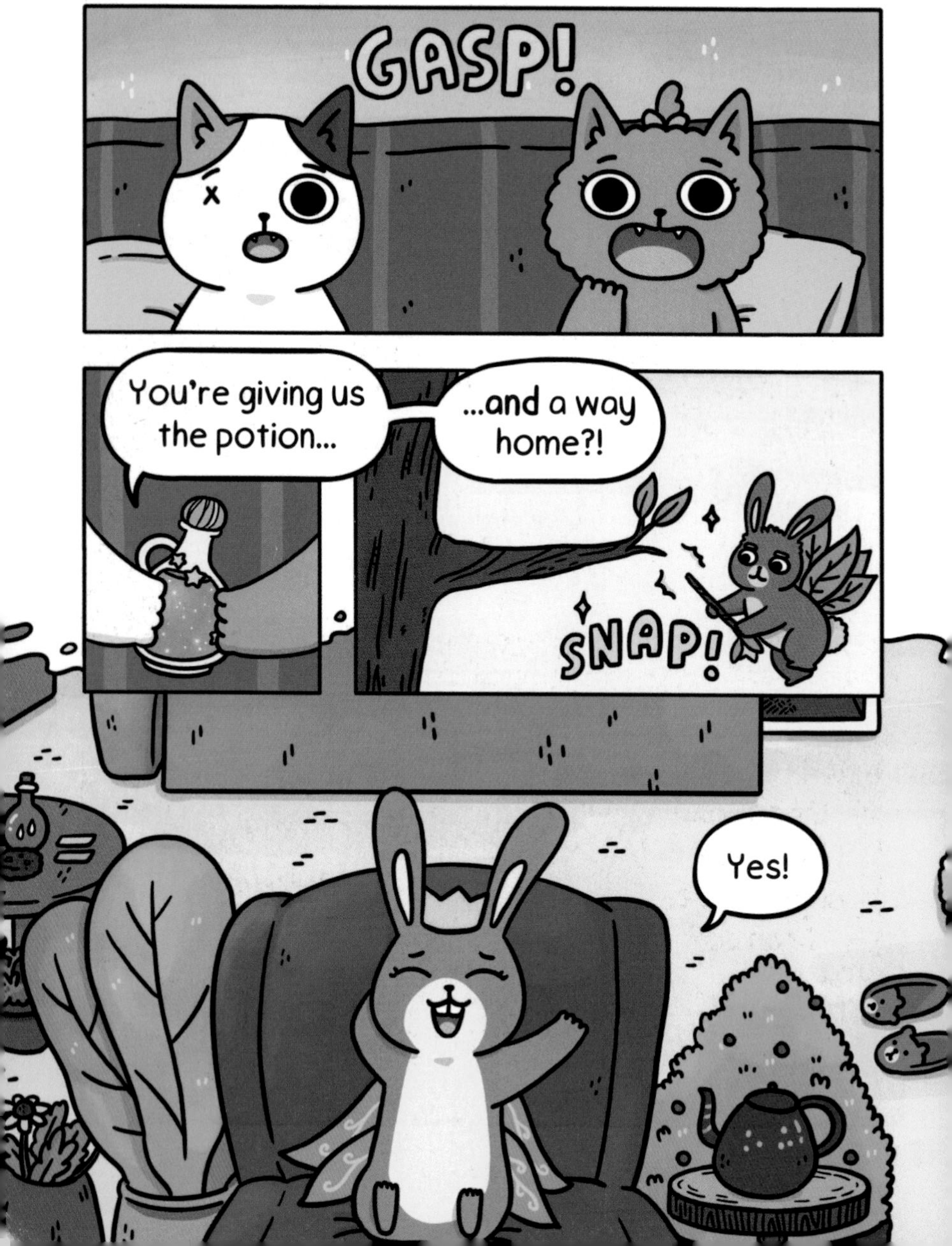
GASP!
You're giving us the potion...
...and a way home?!
SNAP!
Yes!

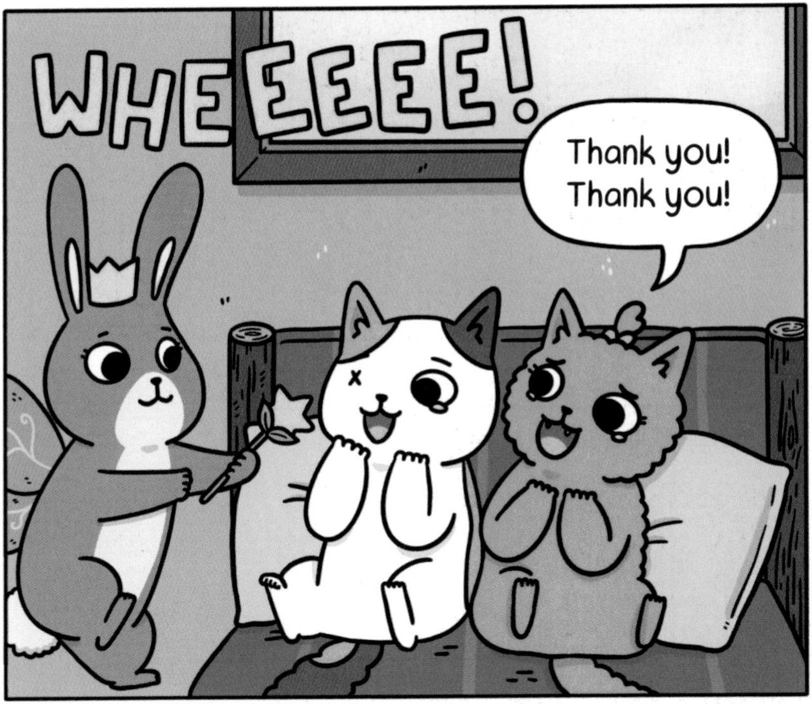
WHEEEEEE!
Thank you! Thank you!

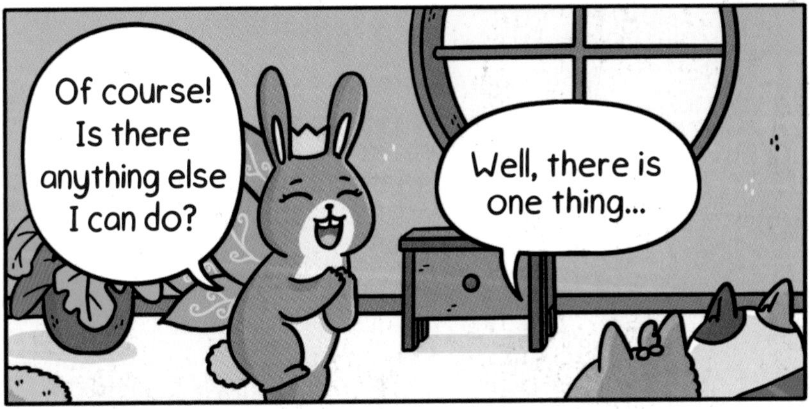
Of course! Is there anything else I can do?
Well, there is one thing...

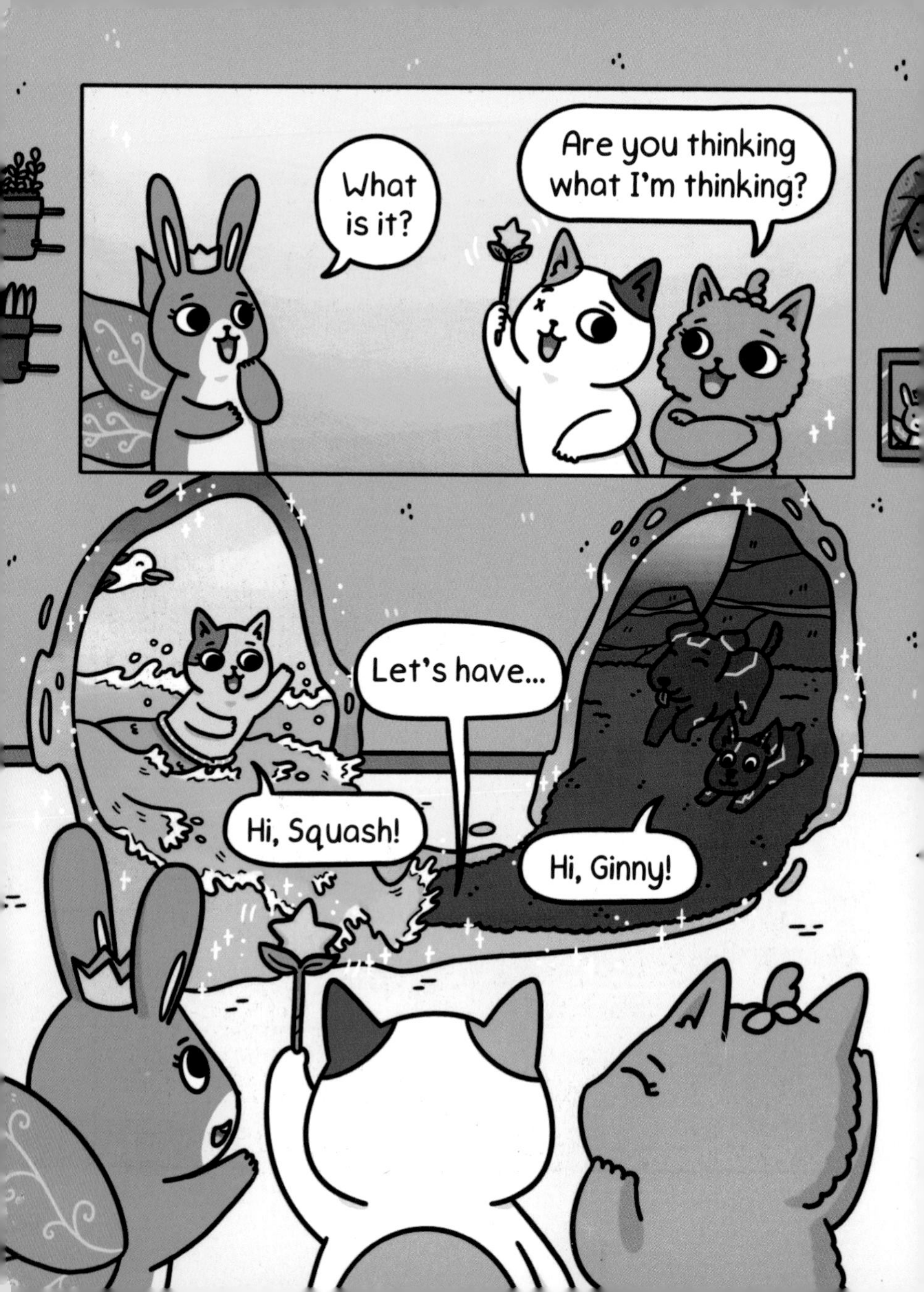
Are you thinking what I'm thinking?
What is it?
Let's have...
Hi, Squash!
Hi, Ginny!

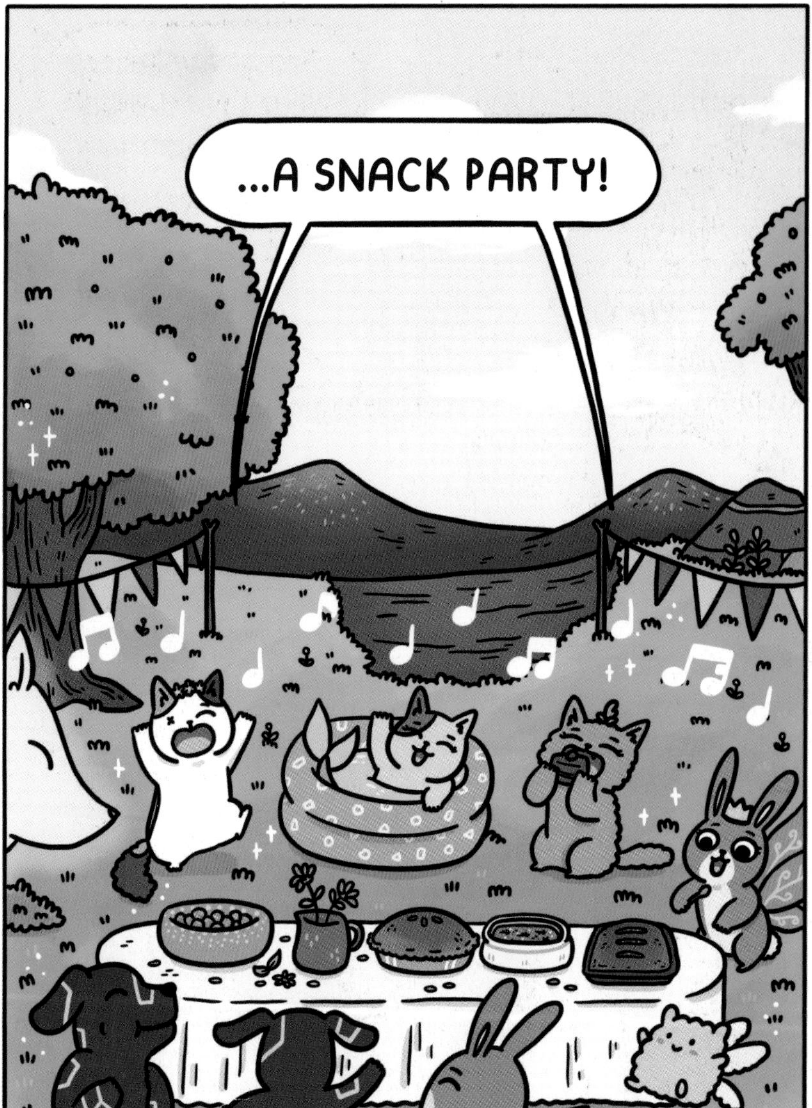
...A SNACK PARTY!

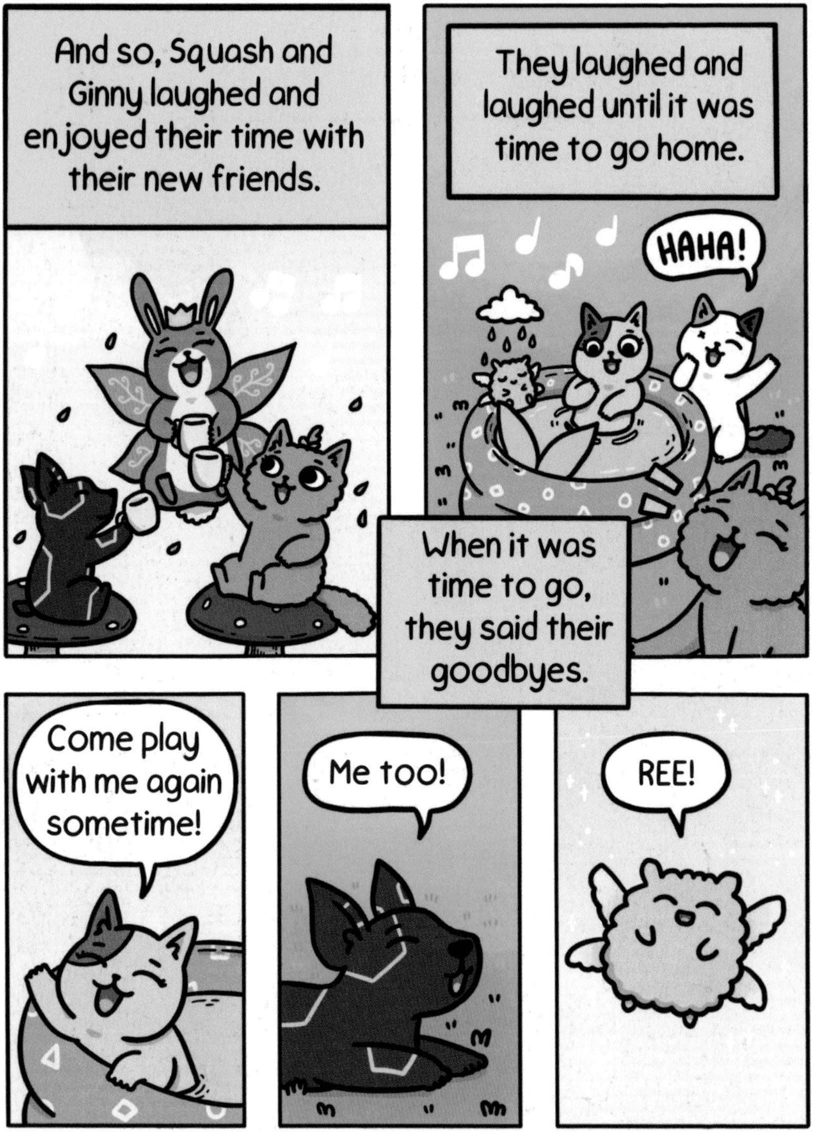
And so, Squash and Ginny laughed and enjoyed their time with their new friends.
They laughed and laughed until it was time to go home.
HAHA!
When it was time to go, they said their goodbyes.
Come play with me again sometime!
Me too!
REE!

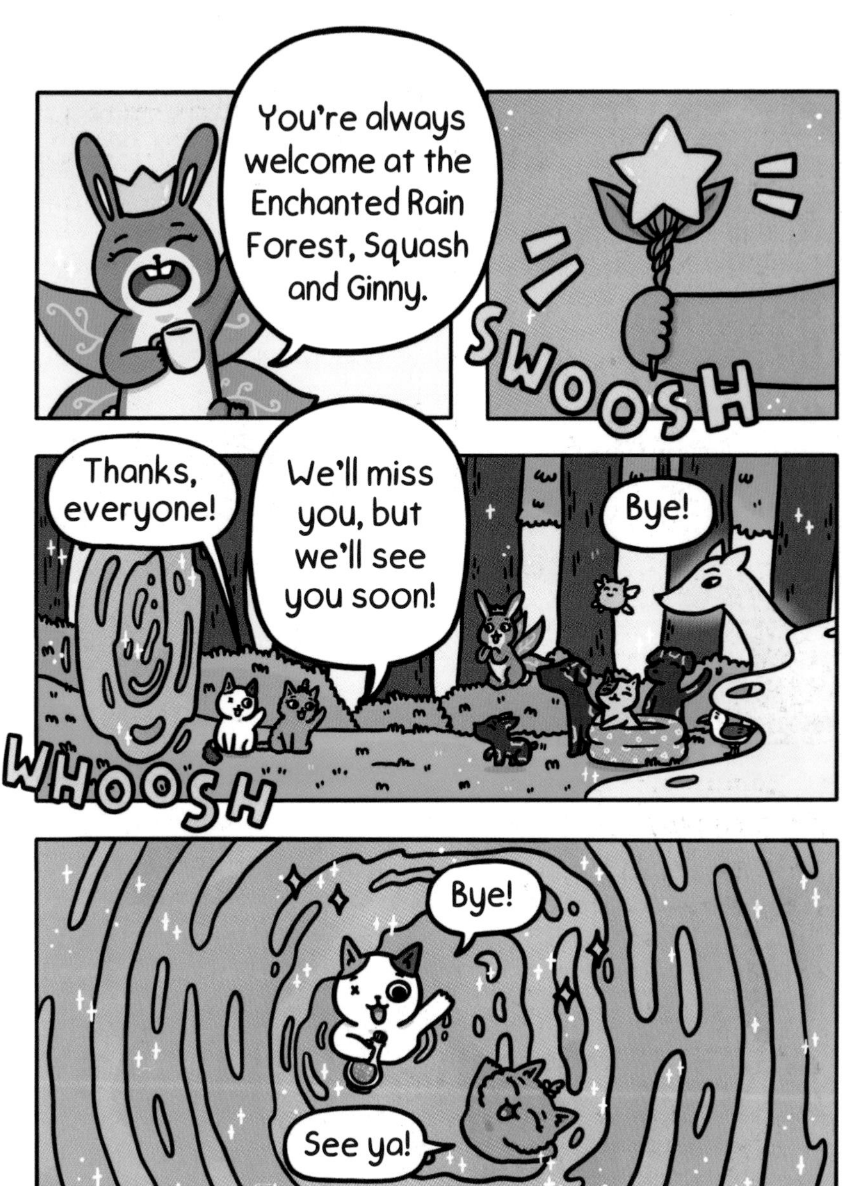
You're always welcome at the Enchanted Rain Forest, Squash and Ginny.
SWOOSH
Thanks, everyone!
We'll miss you, but we'll see you soon!
Bye!
WHOOSH
Bye!
See ya!

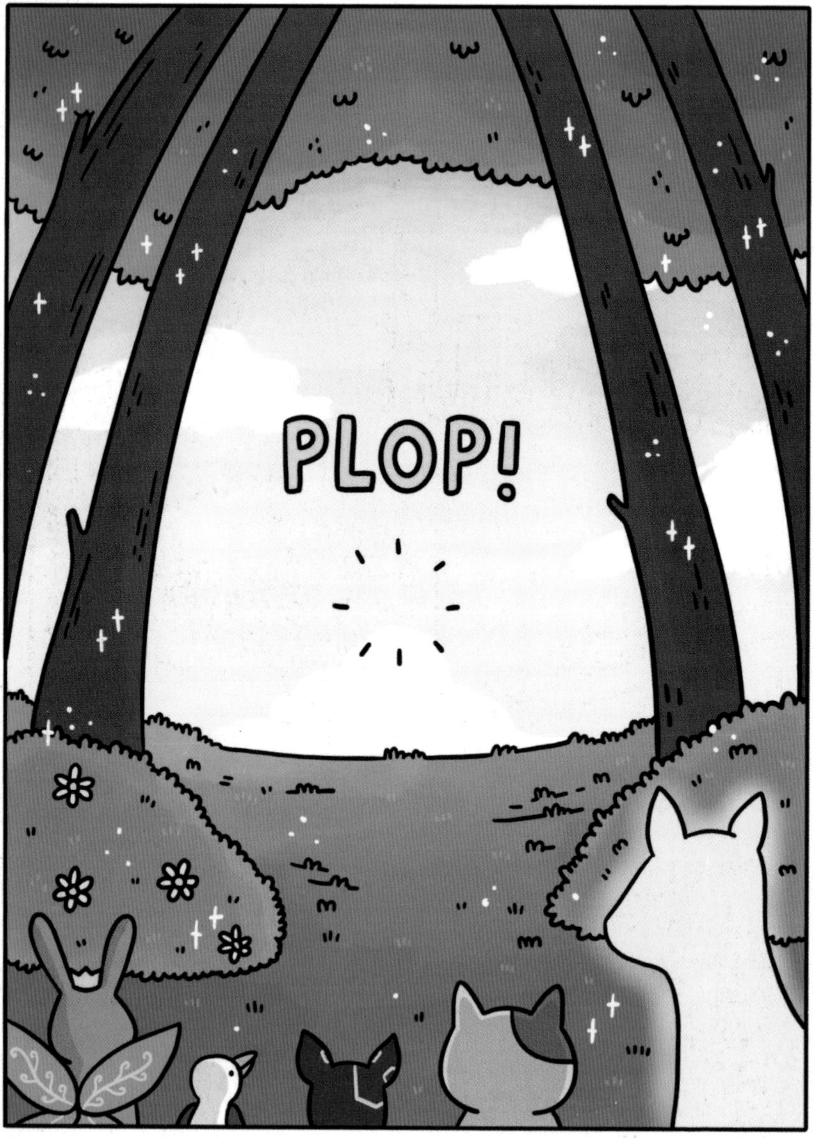
PLOP!

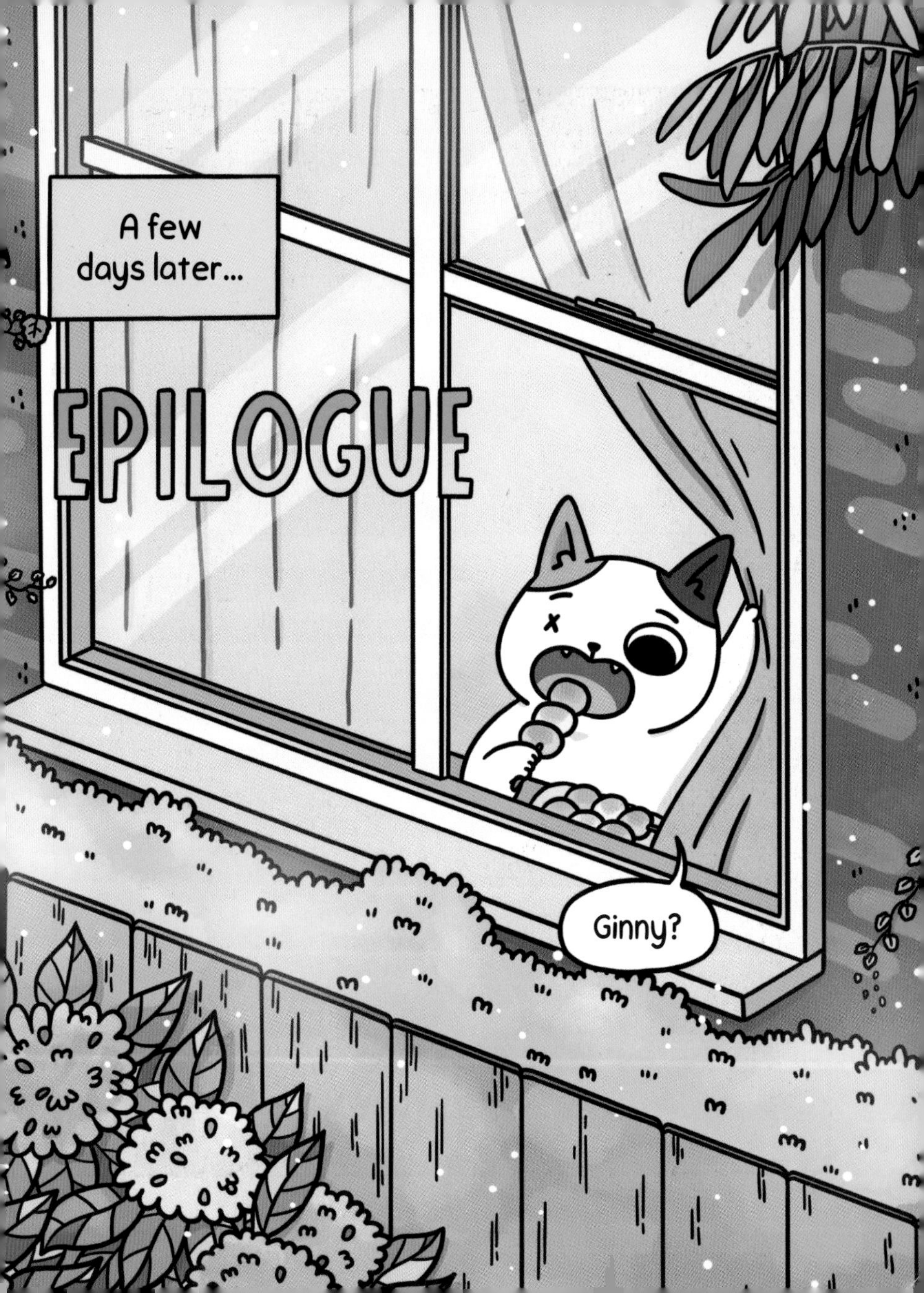
A few days later...
EPILOGUE
Ginny?

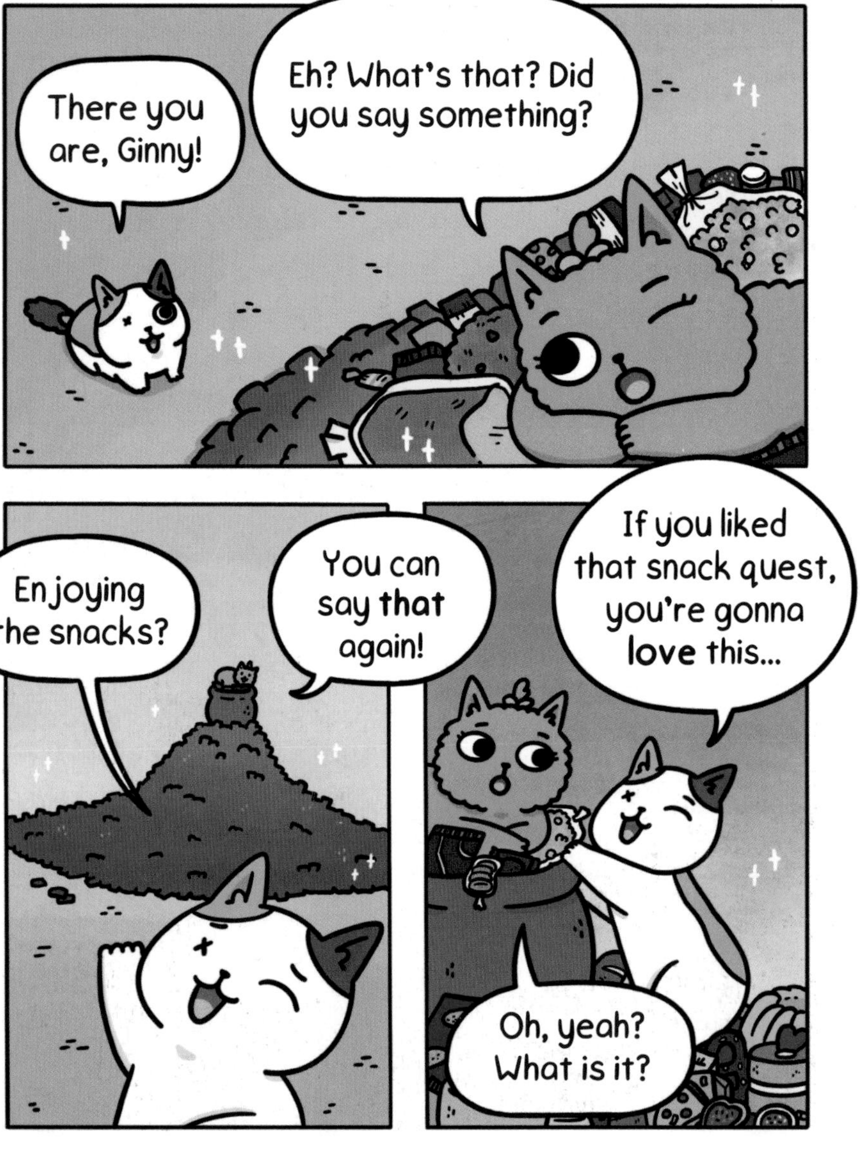
There you are, Ginny!
Eh? What's that? Did you say something?
Enjoying the snacks?
You can say **that** again!
If you liked that snack quest, you're gonna **love** this...
Oh, yeah? What is it?

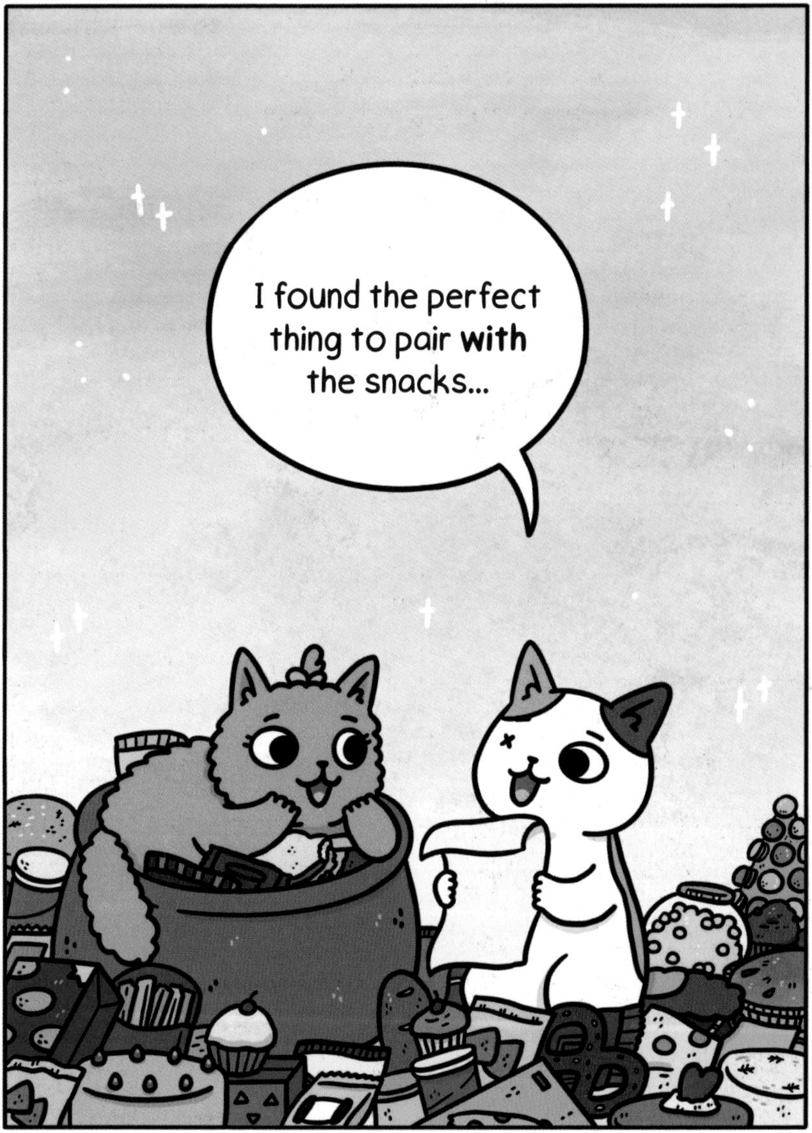
I found the perfect thing to pair **with** the snacks...

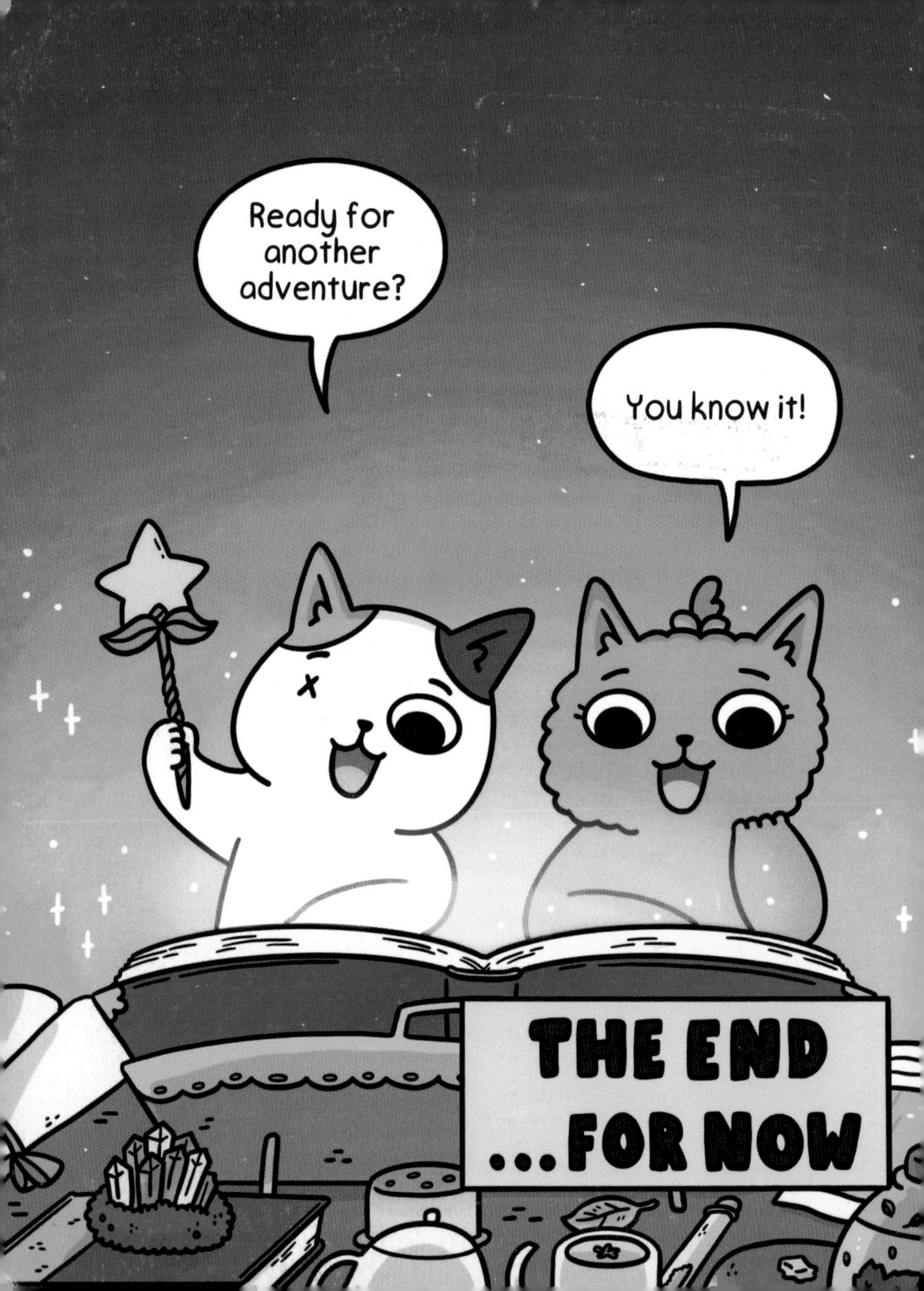
Ready for another adventure?
You know it!
THE END ...FOR NOW